Antonina Irena Brzozowska was born, grew up and educated in the north of England. A former teacher, she has a strong interest in the Polish and Hawaiian cultures and traditions.

To Michael, Thomas and Oliver Carter.
Keep reading.
Stay happy.
Keep smiling!

Antonina Irena Brzozowska

'KING' KAMEHAMEHA

AUSTIN MACAULEY PUBLISHERS™

LONDON ∗ CAMBRIDGE ∗ NEW YORK ∗ SHARJAH

A CIP catalogue record for this title is available from the British Library.

ISBN 9781398433670 (Paperback)
ISBN 9781398433687 (ePub e-book)

www.austinmacauley.com

First Published 2022
Austin Macauley Publishers Ltd®
1 Canada Square
Canary Wharf
London
E14 5AA

Table of Contents

Chapter One

Kamehameha – It's All in the Name!

Kamehameha. Yes, you may well ask. Well, believe me; I was just as bemused, shocked and horrified when my new owner announced, out of the tropical blue, that that particular name was the one I was going to be stuck with for the duration of my doggie years.

"What kind of a crazy name is that?" I heard one of her friends giggle.

Perhaps there was some hope of clemency. My ears pricked up, only to rapidly fall again.

"It's an honourable name. He is to be named after the Great King Kamehameha of Hawaii; I'm hoping some greatness will rub off on my pooch," Toni, my mistress, explained as I sighed miserably and resigned myself to my dismal fate.

I tell you she's nuts, there is no other word to describe her. Ever since she went on a vacation to Hawaii, and even before she set one foot on the tropical paradise, she's been Hawaii mad and now it looks as if I'm going to have to play a part in her insanity.

"No other dog in the world will have the same name, that's for sure." Another friend smiled benevolently at me, before scooping me up in her arms and cooing over me. "He is such a cutie."

I closed my eyes to it all, consoling myself with the thought that there was still a tiny spark of hope; perhaps her friends would make her see sense; perhaps she'll sleep on it and bestow on me a sensible name, a sable and white coloured rough collie, and distant cousin of that gal who starred in those doggie movies, deserves. After all; tomorrow, as they say, is another day.

Chapter Two
Doors, Chairs and Food for Thought

Sadly, the name business was a no-go area. Like everything in her life, I soon learned, once Toni had made up her mind, there was no budging her. Now, this was a good thing in a lot of ways; but not so good in others. Anyway, I was stuck with this unusual name, Kamehameha; although, to Toni's disgust, I was often referred to as 'Maya', 'Kami', 'Come here, come here' and, to her absolute horror, and mine, 'Mayonnaise'!

Anyway, my mind is racing. Let's get back to when my new life started. It was a promising morning as I frolicked with my siblings in our pen, then settled down for a nice, cosy puppy snooze. I was just about to drop off when, suddenly, there was an unexpected commotion at the door. Then a familiar face, with two complete strangers, walked in; one was especially fussy and rather excitable and seemed to be gawping at me in a most peculiar manner as she grinned, cooed and pointed her chubby forefinger directly in my direction. I must admit I was a bit curious as I stared back unblinkingly, rose and, before I knew it, I was placing one small paw in front of the other and approaching this high-strung female. Immediately, she clapped her podgy hands, jumped up and down excitedly taking my approach as some sort of wonderful sign and, before I knew it, my fate was sealed and we were whizzing past fields and noisy motors, tall buildings and small, until we came to a sudden stop.

As I opened my eyes and surveyed my surroundings, I must say, I wasn't too impressed. I seemed to be in a gigantic basket, way too big for a puppy of my size, and all I could hear was a constant flow of words. What my new mistress was saying to me I don't know; though, from her tone of voice, I assumed it was all complimentary. Shortly after, she was accompanied by three other females, all swooning over me, as if I was a delicious piece of roast chicken, patting and stroking me as I desperately wished them all to disappear and leave me in peace;

after all, I had lived through an exhausting and emotional morning; for, not only was I separated from my mother and siblings, I had endured a long journey and was thrust into the unknown, all because I was the cutest of the bunch. But, frankly, I blame myself; if it wasn't for my inquisitive nature, I would still be snoozing in my own bed. That will teach me!

My adoring fans disappeared only for their cooing, stroking and patting to be replaced by a loud burring noise which frightened me half to death. I later learned it was something called a washing machine. Toni had apparently switched it on for my benefit so I could familiarise myself with this monstrosity; that was very thoughtful of her!

Wherever I scanned my inquisitive eyes I saw an abundance of toys and I knew my mistress was trying her utmost best to make me comfortable; but, I missed my mum and it was to get worse. The dark night quickly arrived and I was left with all the doggie comforts a puppy could wish for: a warm, cosy blanket in a spacious basket, lots of toys, a warm water bottle; but no mum, brothers and sisters to cuddle up to.

I had to learn the ways of the world very quickly. I was already intelligent enough to know that rewards, in the form of tasty treats, come with good behaviour; so, all I needed to do was to play by the rules and my life would be quite cushy and the more obedient I became, the more luxurious my life would become. But, first, I had to get rid of some nasty habits and this was not going to be easy; in fact it was, I feared, going to be a somewhat difficult feat to accomplish.

House training, I guessed, was the most important skill to learn and, being an intelligent puppy, I soon caught on that newspapers were laid out, from the foot of my basket to the outside door, for a purpose and not a mere decorative design. Quickly, I twigged on that every time I did a pee or a poo on a piece of newspaper, I would receive a treat. What I couldn't fathom out, at first, was why the newspapers were disappearing and decreasing, from the direction of my basket to the outside door, after every pee or poo; and soon I realised it was time to go into the outside world for such things. I had, of course, already been outside and ventured a little into the garden; but soon ran back inside as fast as my little legs would carry me. I wasn't ready yet. Soon, however, the newspapers disappeared for good and I did my business in the garden and, in due course, beyond the boundaries of the garden.

I was, from the start, an inquisitive type of guy and this curiosity of mine propelled me, hesitantly at first, towards the front gate where I found I could see all kinds of interesting things between the tall metal bars: humans of all ages and sizes, cats crossing the road without a care in the world; but, the noise and speed of tall and small noisy vehicles whizzing by was too much for me and I was soon back inside my new home, safe and sound.

Try as I did, I just could not get used to that oversized doggie basket; for, apart from its size, I didn't like the look or feel of it. Sure, it was nice and soft to sit and lay in; but, it had hard, wooden interwoven sides around me and I just didn't like them; so, every time my owner popped me inside the basket, as soon as her back was turned, I popped right back out again, much to Toni's frustration. That carried on for quite a while; Toni popped me in, I popped out and so on until thankfully, one day, the big basket disappeared and a big soft duvet and cushions were left in its place. Luxury indeed!

Wooden furniture and fixtures; don't get me started on doors and chairs, which are both a blessing and a curse. The problems they caused me were all to do with my pearly whites, or, more to the point, the advent before their full appearance. Nothing on Earth could soothe my itchy gums sufficiently, except the lovely feel of the wooden texture surrounding the bevelled glass doors, one leading from our poky kitchen to the lounge and the other door leading to the hall. I came upon their healing qualities purely by chance, as I rested my head on the ceramic tiles beneath one door. What joy, as I gnawed at the wood without a care in the world, revelling in blessed relief and; so, I gnawed and chewed with all my might, oblivious to everything and everyone when suddenly…

"Kamehameha!"

My little body froze; my gums, with a couple or so of new-born teeth stuck to the delicious wood. I closed my eyes and squeezed them tightly as I awaited my fate; for, somehow, I knew it would not be a treat. Like a solidified statue I sat with my nose firmly stuck to the bevelled glass, not daring to move a muscle, for I was beginning to recognise that stern voice and it was certainly not one of approval and praise, with promise of a reward. I waited and waited, my gums itching and desperate to get back to the medicinal wood but protocol prevailed. While I waited for what was to come my sentence; slowly, I unglued my jaw and intelligent nose from the door and cautiously turned my head around. I so wish I hadn't. The look I encountered was one of black thunder; Toni's usual tranquil face was a threatening cloud ready to explode and I knew, only too well, that the downpour was heading for me.

"Kamehameha!" She sat down on a nearby stool, stood up, sat down again; her thunderous, unblinking eyes directed straight at me as she yelled at the top of her voice, making me quiver like a wobbly jelly. "Look what you have done to my doors… my chairs… You've ruined them… ruined them, you little villain. Get out! Get out!"

There was no point waiting for a chicken strip; one last backward glance at her stormy countenance was quite enough, the door was opened and out I fled. I would, at this point, have fled to the ends of the world, wherever that may be, but, unfortunately, there was no route of escape, all gates were firmly closed. I was a prisoner. Somehow, I managed to scramble under the branches of a large conifer and there I sat, wondering what on Earth I had done and when it would be safe to venture out again. After what seemed an eternity, everything seemed quiet on the home front, but was it safe to make my advance back home? After a lot of thought, I decided to bury myself further into the soothing, camouflage of the Conifer and there I remained.

Minutes turned into hours as a dark blanket descended over everything around. I'd heard Toni call my name, but to be quite honest, I was a little scared to creep out from my hiding place and encounter my mistress, she had seemed so very cross; but, now, I must admit, her voice seemed urgent, a worried tone lacing her words.

"Kamehameha… Kamehameha… where are you? Come on Kamehameha… come on home, Kamehameha…"

Hesitantly, I peered out from beneath the tangled web of bristly branches and saw a pair of feet rushing back and forth, this way and that, as an anxious voice constantly called, "Kamehameha… where are you? Come on… I forgive you… come on home… Kamehameha…"

My little body became a cauldron of indecision, anxiety and worry. I didn't know what to do. On the one hand, what if she was still furious with me? On the other hand, I didn't like the black blanket surrounding me and the distant hooting of some bird, in the woods beyond, didn't thrill me at all. It was all becoming far too scary for my liking.

"Kamehameha… come on home… please…"

The voice, I thought, was becoming more gentle; though, quite urgent in its appeal, and there was something in that last word… maybe I was forgiven. I stuck my head further out. The scurrying feet were turning in my direction. I stuck one cautious paw out from beneath the tangle of lower branches.

"Oh Kamehameha… Kamehameha…"

Suddenly, I was propelled into the air, brought down and showered with kisses and hugs. "Oh Kamehameha," I heard my mistress say, as she buried her head in my soft fur.

Safely back on my duvet, all quiet in my kingdom, I began to understand it all. I have come to the conclusion that every crisis can be turned on to the master, or mistress, leading them to believe it's always their fault. It's up to each pooch, whatever their breed, to weigh and work each calamity out to their advantage and assume the role of the innocent victim, then, and only then, can a pooch resume his, or her, rightful role as Sovereign!

Chapter Three
My Kingdom, My Servant

I have arrived at the favourable conclusion that two can play Toni's game. If I am stuck, she would say honoured, with a regal name then, I am determined to make my home my castle and to be treated like a king.

In my point of view, to be a successful sovereign is to get one's way, in all things, at all times, no matter what. However, I was also beginning to realise that this was not always going to be an easy thing to accomplish; it would, in fact, I feared, be a painstakingly slow, and difficult, challenge for Toni, for, as I have hinted to you, she is set in her ways and, on top of it all, she is a teacher, so she knows something about rules and discipline. I'd have to be cunning and patient if I was to get my way, but I also knew one thing would always win her, and everybody else, over; my good looks. As I have mentioned, I am a rough collie and come from a long line of staunch pedigrees. My beautiful coat is of a sable and white colour. I have white socks, or boots, as I like to call them; I have sad, soulful eyes, ready to melt any tyrant's heart; plus, my normally mild-mannered nature lures any sensible human towards me and I kind of have a smiling mouth which adds to my credit; that is except when I see Toni retrieving the grooming brush and that's another story; so, young and elderly warm to me immediately, treating me with the regal respect I expect and deserve. However, at times, Toni ruffles my fur and sets me off in a spin as you will see in later chapters.

I am only six months old, but already I know all there is to know about treats, and how to get them with the minimal amount of effort on my part. Just looking pretty is my favourite; this requires no work at all and earns me many delicious nibbles.

The house is at my disposal and when Toni's at work, I make the most of my kingdom. Her double bed is my favourite place; so, when I see the outside door close and hear her heals clicking down the stone paving, I know it's time to head for the bed and make myself comfortable for the day. The full-length wardrobe mirror, across the width of one wall, adds to my state of luxury for I can muse at my handsome reflection; but, I can also see Toni coming up the stairs and, so long as she doesn't catch me snoozing on her bed, I'm safe.

The lounge downstairs also serves my purpose well. When Toni is nowhere to be seen, I rub my head vigorously against her plush, white sofa and soon I am in a state of complete relaxation, ready for another snooze.

The kitchen is not so good. It is a poky, dismal area and, when I'm fully grown, I can see there isn't going to be much room for the two of us. One of us will have to go and it certainly isn't going to be me!

So, yes, I feel quite relaxed and happy in my kingdom; though, don't get me wrong, it is not always a blissful oasis. On the rare occasion, when Toni stealthily walks up the stairs and catches me napping on her bed, or, worse still, catches me rubbing my head exuberantly on her sofa, total pandemonium ensues, with a great deal more besides and, my goodness, can she shout for England; really, she has certainly missed her calling as a town crier! In these instances, there is no time to be laid back; it's time to run for your life into the great outdoors and not look back.

Thankfully, she spent a small fortune on the garden a couple of years ago; so, I am always successful in hiding in its vicinity; actually, for a semi-detached property, it's quite spacious and always peaceful as it is situated at the back of the house, with only the fields bordering the wall and gate. I would certainly say the garden is aesthetically pleasing with its abundance of grasses, flowering shrubs, Conifers and mini spruces scattered tastefully around an array of assorted pebbles. Stepping stones weave their way around the garden to the bottom patio, which displays a selection of tall standing spruces as its backdrop. The stepping stones are a blessing and have won me many a treat, for Toni thinks she has installed, in me, a modicum of excellent behaviour as she witnesses me strolling gracefully along them. I don't think she realises, and I'm certainly not going to make it obvious to her, that I use the stepping stones to save my paws and, so far as she's ignorant of the fact and her friends see such intelligent behaviour, I acquire treats and a generous measure of adulation.

The drive is also my territory and woe-betide any stranger who strives to pass through the gate without my say-so, especially if there is no tasty treat in sight.

So, there you have it; a glimpse into my kingdom. Now, as for my servant in the making, Toni is a hard nut to crack. I think she has acquired the misguided opinion that I am her pet pooch and must do what she says at all times. Well, that's what she thinks! However, I must begrudgingly admit, to a certain degree, she is right. She did choose me; she brought me into her home and, so far, has provided me board and lodgings; though, I must say, my noble ancestors are turning in their graves at such common phraseology. Anyway, the long and the short of it is I have to be grateful; or, at least appear to be so. However, Toni made a rod for her own back when she bestowed on me a royal name. That makes all the difference. So, while there is a fine line between respect and autonomy, she has to be allowed to think that she is the boss, whereas, in fact, we all know I'm the king of the castle. This learning curve is a slow process and on-going; it has to be undergone subtly so that Toni does not realise she's being secretly trained into the role of a servant; for, if she has an inkling of my plan there will be no peace and my reign will be over before it has truly begun.

I, of course, have undertaken to guard the house, and its surroundings, with an air of authority over anyone who ventures to cross my path, leading Toni to think I am an excellent guard dog and praises me to the highest heavens; whereas, in fact, everyone sees I am actually in charge, as I allow humans in and out as the whim takes me.

Breakfast time is a pleasurable time. All I have to do is to sit pretty and give my mistress my paw, making her heart melt as she presents me with a thick slice of wholemeal toast spread generously with honey, marmalade; or my favourite, home-made strawberry jam; any three of those three breakfast delights will do as long as it's not that brown, thick stuff humans seem to either love or hate. I had a taste of that stuff once and was sure Toni was trying to finish me off, for one of many past misdeeds she had not forgotten about. Never again! I live in an all-inclusive setting, where food and drink are always there at my disposal and therefore, it is up to me whether I wish to partake of it or not.

Food from Toni's plate is a rare treat indeed; especially after the time I decided to devour her Christmas dinner and ended up on the v—e—t's table and almost through the pearly gates. Remind me to tell you about that episode in a later chapter. On the rare occasion when I do manage to scrounge a piece of tasty roast chicken, I have to give her my paw ten thousand times, but it's well worth the effort. More often than not, she flatly refuses to share her meals; her excuse, I will throw up on one of her precious carpets.

Treats are plentiful, for I have quickly learned valuable techniques to acquire them, without any questions asked. You see, now that I am growing more intelligent by the day, I know that cunning and skilfulness are all that's required in the art of achieving one's heart's desire. Presenting my paw always seems to delight everyone into presenting me some type of treat; sitting down when requested to do so also seems to earn me a tasty morsel; walking sensibly, especially when in view of other humans, earns rewards; greeting their dogs politely; coming inside when I don't particularly want to; all these things earn me a treat; so, on an average day, I don't think I do so badly where treats are concerned; added to the mix, when visitors roll up they usually bear gifts, so long as I allow them through the gate; but obviously, their entrance is up to my discretion; though I flatly refuse to allow any old riff raff through the portals of my kingdom. So all in all, where treats are concerned, I cannot complain.

Of course, I like to be pampered; what level headed pooch doesn't? So, lots of compliments are always welcome; stroking my fur makes me feel relaxed but don't even think about touching the back of my head; that is a no-no if you want to live. Suffice it to say, I show my pearly whites if people don't stop when I've warned them with my flashing eyes. Neither do I find grooming a relaxing pass-time; however, feel free to tickle me behind the ears and under my chin, I'll be your friend forever.

Just to mention, when friends, unsolicited visitors and family come a-calling; however brief the visit, I expect, at all times, to be the centre of attention. Ignore me at your peril!

So, all things considered, I am pretty established here. Both Toni and I know our boundaries. She thinks she's the boss and I allow her to live in her blissful ignorance, knowing full well the identity of the true sovereign.

Chapter Four
Flimsy Laundry and
Oversized Pants

The memory haunts me to this very day and we are talking about seven and a half years after the embarrassing scenario. How Toni can sleep peacefully at night, without being haunted by recurring nightmares, I'll never fathom out for I still have flashbacks about the whole affair.

As I remember, it was a lovely sunny day, an array of colourful T-shirts, tops, leggings and bits of underwear were flapping merrily in the warm morning breeze; the fragrance of the magnolia scented laundry quite intoxicating as I settled down comfortably for my morning nap. Everything would have been all right if Toni had not decided to hang up a second load of washing on the line. I tried with all of my might to be super good as I lay peacefully, not stirring a muscle, with one eye on the colourful pile still in the basket and my nostrils attune to the soft perfume. Suddenly, something inside me snapped and, before I knew what I was doing, I was hastily weaving my way along the stepping stones with a long, silky object trailing delightfully behind me, and behind the scarf, trailed Toni.

"Come back… Kamehameha… just you come back here, at once!" She shouted at the top of her voice, as she almost caught up with me.

I stopped in my tracks, turned, observed and assessed the situation. Instinct determined the matter and I was on the move again, only just out manoeuvring Toni for she was a pretty sprightly gal when she put her mind to it. I ran and ran, up and down the garden, with joy pounding in my young heart; for what a fun game this was turning out to be.

I could tell Toni was enjoying herself as she ran up and down after me. I turned to evaluate my mistress's progress in her quest and just happened to see her stern, red face which, now I was surmising, was none too pleased. I turned and ran and… ran… until I could run no more. I; or rather, my silky object, was firmly entangled in the prickly needles of the Scots pine. Being of firm, determined stock a slight entanglement was not going to deter me in my pursuit of happiness. I headed back to the laundry basket and, in seconds, my teeth firmly clutched a blouse. I was down at the bottom of the garden, chewing merrily and making delightful little holes in the satin-like material, when Toni finally caught up with me, retrieved the item, wagged her finger in front of my nose and disappeared. This was fun of the highest calibre and, before I knew it, I had kidnapped another article of clothing.. Toni was joining in the fun again, engaging in a delightful Tug of war game, before retrieving the items and putting them back into the basket. What a superb game!

The fourth attempt failed to follow the same rule the last three garments enjoyed. Once more, I sneaked up to the basket, this time snatching an odd-looking garment with holes in the most peculiar places and of a general hideous nature and, may I tell you, most distasteful to the discerning eye. (Yuk!). Still, I thought, what can possibly go wrong? I clenched the pants firmly in my pearly whites for, by now, the routine was well and truly established in my mind and I dashed down the stepping stones at top speed. This time Toni was too involved with hanging the last of the laundry on the line, before engaging in a full-blown gossiping session with our neighbour, and I was left to my own devices. By nightfall, the laundry was safely inside, Toni was tucked up in bed and I was happily dreaming of new adventures.

And so, the days passed dreamily by; 'dreamily', of course, being the operative word. The days continued to be hot and sultry; but, being the intelligent pooch I am, I could tell something was stirring in the air. Sure enough, I was proved right, as usual. The evening was oppressive with an eerie stillness and in the distance I could hear the rumble of thunder; horrible looking black clouds were swiftly gathering in the sky and the rumblings increased in both number and volume. My finely tuned senses told me that whatever was stirring, it was getting nearer as the eerie stillness was replaced by a rushing type of sound. I watched, mesmerised, as a few dead wild cherry leaves, fragile twiglets and other bits of garden debris twirled and whirled around and around, as if performing some crazy dance. The jagged, zigzagged, orange flash of light, followed by deafening blasts of thunder, sent my little legs running at top speed for the safety and sanctuary of home and there, I curled up in a ball, praying for a swift end of the world. My prayer went unanswered and finally, when the sporadic streaks of light and fierce crackling thunder subsided, I slowly uncurled myself and cautiously, with one paw hesitantly placed in front of the other; I made my way to a window and became fascinated by the huge drops beating wildly on the small pebbles outside. Hypnotised, I watched the relentless rain pounding on the grasses making them drab and limp; I watched it beat down on the Scots pine, which stood proud and unyielding, to whatever life threw at it; my eyes straying to the filigree leaves of the Conifers where, as if by magic, the raindrops changed into sparkling, clear dangling jewels. As I watched, enchanted by these shiny diamonds, something, I could not tell what, fluttered briefly in the corner of my eye. I turned my head and I saw… I blinked hard and opened my eyes; this time the vision was more horrifying. I stared at the familiar sight, for how could one mistake them for something else? Once seen, never forgotten; but, what to do now was another problem altogether. There they were a large pair of oversized pants; enough to put any man off women for the rest of his time in this world… and the next. There they were! I still couldn't believe what I was seeing. I blinked once… twice; but, the same ghastly image remained. They were, let me tell you, hanging on a large pole in our neighbour's garden, flapping happily away for the entire world to see. I closed my eyes tightly; sighing deeply, for what can a pooch do in this beastly predicament? I knew, for a fact, Toni was not going to be an ecstatic bunny when things were brought to light; that's if she would survive the shame of it all, for my Toni is rather a quiet, private type of person and, to be honest, I'm not quite sure if she would see the funny side of things. I, myself, was beginning to feel uneasy and quite disturbed about the whole incident as black thoughts seeped into my mind, for the stark possibility of treats diminishing; or, indeed, disappearing altogether, not to mention the possibility of ending up homeless did not thrill me at all.

And so, I kind of attempted to distract her in any which way I could think. First, it was yapping. Now, I was always pretty good at yapping back to her when she spoke to me, she always thinking it was some kind of weird human-doggie type of conversation (I told you she was nuts!). In the past, this always distracted her and, I'm pleased to say, it worked this time until she decided to stop our conversation mid flow and dispatch the inside rubbish into the outside bin. No… no… no… this would not do. She would, I knew with a hundred percent certainty, immediately spot the offending article; because, let me tell you, she's got the eyes of a hawk, and then my life would not be worth living for I knew she would surely pin the blame on me. Quickly, I grabbed her new slipper and a new battle ensued. And, so it was, she was saved from humiliation… at least for a few hours.

The hours slipped by and with them, the evening slipped into night. Toni was preparing some kind of lesson plans for the following school week, I was by her feet snoozing and everything was right in the world; then, she stirred, I stirred and eased back into my cosy position, vowing nothing was going to move me for a couple of hours or so. Soon, thoughts of how I was going to capture the neighbour's cat filtered through my sleepy mind.

"A—a—ah!"

Eyes stark open, I felt every strand of my fur stand on end, my ears immediately pricking up at the ready.

"A—a—ah!"

This, I thought, does not bode well. Should I… shouldn't I… should I go to see what on Earth was causing all this commotion that was disturbing my beauty sleep? Instinct was the decider. Like a Jack-in-the-box, I sprang up from my comfortable niche and was by my mistress's side in a flash. All we could see from our vantage point, out the small kitchen window, was something white fluttering this way and that in the darkness of the gloomy, stormy night.

"It's a—a—g-gho-st," I heard her mumble before she shrank from the window.

Of course, with my high intelligence, I knew at once what she was staring at and it most certainly was not a ghost; though I so wish it was!

Before I knew what was happening, she hastily stuffed some belongings into a bag, scooped me up, and ran out the door. In less than fifteen minutes, we were whizzing down the motorway, heading for the sanctuary of her sister's house.

The next morning sealed my fate. For the next two days; and, it's too depressing for me to work those out in doggie days, there were to be no more treats of any sort, until my mistress had recovered from her shame and humiliation; for, you see, she had finally taken the rubbish out into the disposal bin outside when, eyes aghast, she spotted, and stared, at the long pole and, as her eyes rose, there waving for all the world, and immediate neighbours, to see were her favourite oversized pants. Attempts to smuggle them back played on her mind, but to no avail. A door opened, a beaming elderly neighbour stepped out and enquired politely, with a twinkle in his eyes. "Are these, by any chance, yours, Miss Lublinska?"

She closed her eyes, squeezed them tightly and nodded her head, unable to utter a word. Suffice it to say, for the next week she avoided all neighbours and I was well and truly in the dog house!

Chapter Five
The String of Polish Sausages Episode

I need to inform you, at this stage, that Toni, my mistress, hails from Polish extraction and therefore, one way or another, there's a Polish influence in the house, for example, the conversation between herself and her kin is strange, to say the least. I, and everybody else tuning in, will hear two different languages, sometimes three, when she's in one of her strange moods and decides to sprinkle in a little bit of traditional Hawaiian (I'll get back to her obsession with that particular part of the world sometime later). Anyway, anyone listening to a conversation between Toni and her siblings will, in most cases, only be able to understand the English bit of the conversation; or, gossip as it usually turns out to be, which is quite frustrating to the nosey eavesdropper as she rabbits on in English and her kin in Polish. I mean, honestly, how weird is this? However, I'm proud to announce, I am a rare breed of dog who understands both languages and some Hawaiian! I am, as you have probably fathomed out, a pretty clever hound, as I am bilingual, begrudgingly learning Hawaiian as my third language. Anyway, going back to the Polish influence. The Polish food, I must admit, is rather good and, I must say, I am rather partial when it comes to the poppy seed cake; though the seeds sometimes get stuck in my pearly whites but the delicious, sweet taste is well worth the sacrifice. Now, as for the Polish sausage, that is my absolute favourite. These sausages come in all sizes and tastes and when my nose sniffs out the long, dry, spicy kabanos, my whole body thrills at the anticipation of a tasty bite. I have seen humans eat the kabanos on its own, with raw onion, in salads and sandwiches; in other words, it's very versatile. I have tasted morsels when Toni has been generous enough to throw some my way or when I'm off my food she has enticed me back to it with a little of the delicious stuff. It never fails. I must admit I have deceived her and feigned illness on more than one occasion; I fear now she is cottoning on to my treachery!

The incident happened one evening when Toni had prepared a delicious looking salad; well, delicious in her opinion; personally, I wouldn't look twice at the ghastly looking thing, especially as there is no sight, or whiff, of any meat on the plate. However, things changed rapidly and for the better, for my mistress sensibly added two delicious pieces of kabanosy to her unappetisingly, boring rabbit food on her plate. I could only sit, stare, smell and dream only, this time, my dream became reality, for as I was musing about the possibility of a tasty morsel, the phone interrupted my pleasant daydream. My eyes briefly followed my mistress as she sauntered into the hall, and darted back to the delightful kabanosy within reaching distance. Etiquette prevailed and any thoughts of stealing temporarily put aside. And all would have been well if she had returned to her plate instead of sitting down and partaking in a hearty session of juicy gossip. I mean, how much can a pooch, even of my calibre, endure? And, this certainly was becoming an enduring challenge beyond reason. Begrudgingly, I unstuck my eyes from the plate and watched her tuck her feet underneath her as she chin-wagged for England. Well, I thought, if she had abandoned her post, then I cannot be held responsible for what happens. I nudged further towards the plate. How spicy and tasty it smelled; saliva was already trickling down my face and I couldn't stop myself from nudging a little further and further until my long nose was touching the dish. I could see the dry, knotted end of the long, thin kabanos; I could almost taste its meaty, smoky flavour and feel its chewy texture in my mouth. It was peeping back at me so invitingly and enticingly; I nudged further still. Snap! I was chomping away at the tasty titbit, though hardly enough for a growing pup like myself. Snap… snap and the kabanos was fast disappearing. Not to worry, there was another one begging to be eaten. Within seconds, it was inside my tummy and I was secretly congratulating myself on my clever mission when I spotted the open packet and, to my sheer delight, out peeped more enticing sausages. In my stomach they went, as quick as a flash. To be honest with you, when I got to the seventh one, I was debating with myself whether indeed I should leave it. Common sense prevailed, for when was I going to get another lucky opportunity to partake in such a delightful feast? And so, the last kabanos was soon firmly tucked away in my tummy, making me feel very happy and contented. I heard footsteps approaching; my belly full, I was only too relieved to slouch away on to my duvet and snooze it all off. Before I slipped into a pleasant dream, I heard Toni mumbling to herself. "Well, I'm bowled over! Where on Earth have the kabanosy got to? I'm absolutely sure they were here… I must be losing my marbles." Losing your marbles to place them in reach of a dog's jaw, I thought. Ah, well, least said, soonest mended. I relaxed into blissful sleep. It was short lived. I opened one eye a little to notice Toni scurrying this way and that, her head poking in the fridge and into cupboards as a look of total bewilderment etched her puzzled face. There was tension in the air and I knew my mistress was not a happy bunny, for she had set her heart on that 'delicious' salad and certainly not on losing her star ingredients. From her stern, determined look, I knew she was not going to give up easily and sure enough…

"Kamehameha!"

My eyes firmly closed, not a muscle of my body moving, I decided to play deaf and dumb.

"Kamehameha, have you taken my kabanosy?" She stood arms akimbo, resembling old Mother Hubbard when she found her bare cupboard. I could feel her accusing eyes boring into my back, making my fur stand on end, as I desperately hoped I was not giving myself away. Instinct told me to get up, take steps, settle in a corner where she could not see me and bury my guilty head in my paws, but try as I did, I could not obliterate the sound of her pacing up and down; no doubt searching for her kabanosy, which were now beginning to digest nicely in my tummy. After a while, the tension in my body eased and disappeared, for there was insufficient evidence to point the finger at me. Toni had decided she had gone stark raving mad and so the episode ended, or so I thought.

By now, I honestly thought I had gotten away with the theft Scott free. Toni had found a replacement for her kabanosy; from what seemed like thin air, came the Krakowska, another spicy sausage and this time, in her state of total disarray, she threw into my bowl a very generous helping. Saliva, once again, made its familiar journey down my face and, in a flash; I was at my food, digging out the tasty pieces. What a feast!

"Kamehameha; you thief!"

The words hit me like a thunderbolt. I froze like an immortalised image made of marble as a delicious morsel dropped out of my mouth back into the bowl. Slowly, I turned, my eyes, involuntarily staring at the empty kabanos wrapper in Toni's hand. Time stood still.

Suffice it to say, I was allowed no treats the following day. However, I sighed contentedly, that was a small price to pay for the unexpected privilege of banqueting in the style of a king.

Chapter Six
Fireworks Galore

I must have been in Toni's care about two or three months when I first started hearing the terrifying bangs, blasts and long shrill whistles. The thing is, I never knew where they were coming from, where they were going, when to expect them, how long they were going to last or whether they were going to hurt me, or worse still, if they had the potentiality of cutting short my young, pampered life. I knew they were nothing to do with Toni; for, sometimes, she had not arrived from work and I heard the odd, unexpected bang, whizz or whistle; or, indeed, all three, which left my fur standing on end; not to mention my heart thumping, feeling it was about to explode, along with whatever it was that was causing my distress. Whenever these frightening incidents occurred, I froze instantly, not able to move a muscle, my eyes glued to whatever it was I was looking at, the time of the bang, whizz or whistle. I would stand motionless for what would seem an eternity and only after long minutes, when no further minor explosions took place, my young and terrified body would start to relax a little; first, my eyes would become unstuck and look cautiously around, then my spine would slowly release from its hunched stance and, finally, I would begin to move my head and I would begin to get back to my normal self, until the next incident when the whole process would repeat. I noticed that as days and weeks passed, these horrible, strange noises seemed to increase both in number and duration, though their increasing familiarity did not make me feel any more relaxed. Toni, however, seemed to be both oblivious and totally unaffected by the whole process as she clattered around the poky kitchen; even when she sat down to her school work, no amount of banging, whizzing, whirling, whooshing or whistling seemed to stir her; so, I guessed it was safe, though I still refuse to add this experience to my bucket list. Nothing, however, prepared me for what I was to experience in the impending future and the adventure I was to encounter!

As I have mentioned, at that time I was still a young and very impressionable pup. I was not allowed to go out independently into the big, wide world; indeed, I was only allowed to venture into the vicinity of our garden; something, I think, to do with some sort of injections I needed before I could endeavour to branch out. That was okay with me; after all, at that stage in life what I didn't know about the outside world, I didn't miss. Anyway, one dark evening, at the start of November, when all was quiet outside, Toni and I went into our garden for our usual evening stroll though it was, I thought, a little earlier than usual. The evening was still and calm, with just a light breeze rustling the dead autumnal leaves, which were randomly scattered around the garden. I loved stepping over them, for they were like a carpet, feeling soft and squishy under my paws. I was kind of thinking of my evening nap and how comfortable and cosy I would soon be, when… suddenly, Heaven and Earth seemed to open as chaos rained down on Toni and myself in the form of red, blue, purple, green, white and yellow colours; flashing here, there and everywhere; whizzing and banging; screeching, whistling and exploding. I raised my head a little and saw all kinds of beautiful patterns: straight lines and zigzags, circles, stars, flowers interweaving and decorating the black, velvet sky; the noises becoming louder and shriller; nearer and nearer. For long seconds, my paws stuck to the ground, unable to move this way or that, my stark eyes raised to the colourful exhibition could only stare unmoving, unblinking at the wonderful, if somewhat frightening, show and I was mesmerised, lost in a magical world of colour, shape, sounds and even smells. I felt Toni tug at my lead as she attempted to urge me back inside. Begrudgingly, I turned my head to her, about to place one paw in front of the other and follow her lead. Whirr… whizz… bang! Whoosh!! I was gone, as fast as my little legs would carry me, my lead trailing behind me. Where I was heading I did not know; I did not care as I headed past the dark, skeletal trees and the ghostly silhouetted spruces and grasses.

"Kamehameha!" I heard Toni shout amidst the frenzied commotion overhead. "Kamehameha…" I did not stop; did not dare to turn my head, my heart thumping and banging, as I gathered more speed and continued to flee as I headed for the sanctuary of, what I thought was, an easily accessible bush; what kind I could not have identified at that particular time. To my utter dismay, as I tried to force my podgy body into its thickness, I found it rather prickly and not to my liking at all. Still, needs must, I solemnly concluded as I pressed further, an unfriendly needle of some sort sticking into my paw. Further and further I squeezed; deeper and deeper through the bristles and thorns I pushed. At last, there seemed to be a small clearing… the clearing became larger and, before I knew it, I was out in the open field. I was free!

Cautiously, I peered this way and that, seeing only thick blackness before, above and around me. Everything now was still and silent once more. The explosions had stopped and, for a brief moment, I thought about squeezing myself back through the rough, prickly bushes and making my apologetic way home; my brain, however whispered to me, at that very moment, that this was my chance to explore the big, wide world. Sore, I was scared; terrified, to be honest; but, as all great adventurers are frightened to some extent, if they are worth their salt and so, with this belief firmly set in my mind, I set off; I didn't know where; anywhere, I guess, my little paws would take me.

Soon a thick, cool sheet covered everything like a heavy blanket. Sheds, garages and all the houses around seemed trebled in size and very scary looking as they stood looking haunted, disfigured and ugly in their nightly disguise. Stealthily, I put one paw in front of the other, looked directly ahead and walked on. Thoughts of my cosy duvet, the warmth and comfort of my home, not to mention, the endless supply of food pervaded my head; instantly, I dismissed these alluringly attractive thoughts, my paws gathering speed and my mind with a deep resolve to be the intrepid, brave explorer I was destined to be. After what seemed like time immemorial, I sat down and carefully surveyed my surroundings. Everything around me, and beyond, was so still, quiet and peaceful, making my body relax a little. From goodness only knows where, the sudden, unexpected whizzing sound became louder and shriller with each second, making my feet scurry as fast as they could to find shelter under some kind of unrecognisable tree, which had long ago lost all its leaves. A further distant bang was followed by a series of other bangs and whistles all of varying decibels, producing a spectrum of delightful colours and patterns. They now seemed to be increasing in number and frequency, causing a series of gasps, shouts, sighs and screams from the human population. As for me, I knew I had to find a more secure shelter; for this temporary shelter was doing my ears no good whatsoever, and I kind of knew that this spectacle was going to go on for some time to come. Finally, when the chaotic mayhem above seemed to subside a little, I took my cue and eased my way out from beneath the tangled branches and eventually, and to my immense relief, found my way into my own back garden and there I stayed, secretly vowing that nothing in this world would ever entice me out again.

Meanwhile, in the midst of the whirling, banging, whistling, whirring and sizzling mayhem, Toni was beside herself. From my sanctuary of a rather friendly bush, with not too many prickles, I heard her shout my name; her voice becoming more louder, shriller and more urgent with each passing minute; but, as much as I felt for my mistress's obvious distress, no way was I about to venture out from the relative safety of my shelter. My eyes followed her feet as they paced up and down the garden, noting her total disrespect for the rules regarding the stepping stones, as she erratically walked over the crunching gravel, her oversized coat flapping in the night breeze, her eyes peering here and there as she shouted and attempted to cajole me into joining her. No fear, I thought, I'm not that mad!

Actually, I eventually found a relatively comfortable position and began to enjoy the display with its colourful kaleidoscope of stars, flowers, zigzags and interlocking patterns, I couldn't even begin to describe to you. Sadly, to this very day; and we're talking of eight years after that particular eventful night, I haven't got used to the noise accompanying the wonder of this annual show.

A few hours later, after I had miraculously managed to somehow have a snooze, I realised that all the sounds had died away, with only one or two distant bangs and whizzes as witnesses to the evening's former glory. Opening my sleepy eyes, I noticed Toni was accompanied by another human and I immediately recognised the familiar voice as belonging to Mister Frobisher, our elderly neighbour. My mistress had obviously rallied for help to find me and now they were both calling out for me, their eyes darting under bushes and behind trees in their desperate quest to find me. My mind buzzed, working overtime. What do I do? Do I crawl out from my hiding place and risk being punished, or do I stay put? I opted for the latter option; for, my quick thinking, super intelligent brain told me that if I played the victim, it could very well work to my advantage; and I was proved right.

After hours of painstakingly searching the neighbours' gardens, the vicinity of the neighbourhood and beyond, they decided on one last look around our garden. I curled into a tight ball and buried my head, trying to look as petrified as I could, for it would not do at all to give the game away at this stage of the proceedings. My plan worked.

Finally, I heard footsteps approaching, I saw a body bend. I buried my head deeper into my tummy and waited…

"I've found him, Miss Lublinska!" Mister Frobisher bent down further, cursing his joints, and picked me up in his strong hands. "He seems none the worse for wear, as far as I can see," he added, the bag of potential treats disappearing before my very eyes, as I saw him smiling down at me, bringing me closer to himself as he cuddled me and I buried my head deeper into the rough grooves of Mister Frobisher's coat. Suddenly, my ears pricked as I heard Toni's excitable voice.

"Oh, my poor might; I'll never forgive myself." The bag of potential treats returning back on the scene as she scooped me into her arms, profusely showering our neighbour with thanks and me with kisses and cuddles, as she brought me back into the safety and warmth of our home. "Tomorrow," I heard her say, "I'll buy you the tastiest treat I can find." My heart leaped.

That evening, I tucked into a delicious cut of succulent steak which, incidentally, Toni had saved for her own tea; after which I settled down on my luxurious duvet, dreaming of my colourful adventure into the outside world and the tasty treat to come tomorrow.

Chapter Seven
Rules, Regulations and
the 'Sergeant Major'

It was a little time after the Bonfire Night incident that I noticed changes in our domestic set-up; subtle changes at first, hardly noticeable really, but Toni, I realised, was a cunning dame and, like a seasoned magician, she weaved her magic skilfully. I had sensed that she had been trying to instil a new brand of discipline for a while; for she had made it blatantly obvious that things had to be changed. The words I heard her bandy around to Auntie Anusia were: "… he gets away with murder… he thinks he's got me twisted around his little paw… he thinks he's the king of the castle…" I kind of agree with these rather harsh statements; however, phrases such as: "… he's got to learn… I'm the boss…" and the last two: "… I'm thinking of taking him to a dog training school… withdrawing treats…" made me feel positively queasy and sent me on a verge of inner despair. And, of course, the sterner tone she was adapting, the wagging finger and disapproving looks did nothing to make me feel calm, cool and collected.

I guess, I knew I had it coming, for even though I say so myself, I am not the run of the mill, model pooch; but then, what does one expect when I'm issued with a royal name? For, as anyone with a grain of intelligence knows, that a royal name brings with it an automatic royal status and instant immunity from punishment, or at least that's the protocol I am led to believe in. Anyway, as I was saying, I sort of disregarded some rules at my own discretion; silly rules in my book as I am sure you will agree. For example, who on Earth heard of a pooch's paw being wiped on entrance to his abode? Now, if it was a matter of a quick wipe, I would grin and bear it, but Toni rubs them, inspects them, and rubs them again; it's a wonder she doesn't polish them. Only when she is one hundred percent satisfied, there isn't a speck visible to her observant eye, will she allow me to venture forth. Now, I do try and sneak inside, and avoid all this unnecessary fuss, but she always catches me in the act; for, as we know, she's got eyes at the back of her head.

Then, there is this nonsense of the morning greet. A simple 'Good morning' or 'Hi' will not do; it has to be Hawaiian style. "Aloha, Kamehameha," she would hearken chirping in a far too cheerful voce for my liking, at the crack of dawn and, only when I present her with my paw, will she dream of giving me my morning treat. Incidentally, not even a word of thanks for guarding our castle all night!

As I grew up and matured into an adult, and we now venture further into the world beyond the boundaries of our garden, it is not enough for me to stand still at a kerb to allow passing motorists their right of way; she insists on a full sit and patient waiting performance. While this rigmarole delights some discerning motorists and, I must admit, I get a kick from their surprised expressions, I don't see why I should have to sit while Toni stands.

As for treats; well unlike my mistress, I believe I should receive one every five minutes just for being beautiful, intelligent, 'obedient' and for putting up with Toni, but before I can even think of digging my pearly whites into a chicken tit-bit, I have to not only sit, but also present her my paw.

Now that she has made her lounge, which leads from the kitchen and from the staircase, into an open plan setting, would you believe if I told you that I am not allowed past the kitchen door? I mean, would any present-day monarch be happy to reside in the servant's quarters? I think not. This is the least of my problems, next year she's threatening to modernise our kitchen. Heaven only knows where I'll end up!

I have to dine out of porcelain bowls which, I guess, my contemporaries can only dream about. Personally, as long as I have food, who cares whether the bowls are plastic, throw away or anything else? Oh, and only dry food is provided. The odour of canned food is not to my mistress's liking, never mind that I may find the contents delicious, given half the chance.

Grooming is a very sore issue. All I'm going to say about it here is that Toni and I are in a state of war about it and neither of us, it seems, will be claiming victory anytime soon.

Then there are the meets and greets I have to perform when family and friends come a-calling. What a palaver! However, I do get treats, praise and a certain amount of adulation for my efforts, so, I guess I can put up with this unnecessary nonsense.

I think I've mentioned the stepping-stones in the garden in a previous chapter, so I won't dwell on these; just to say, it does not work in my favour if I happen to stray off them; however, I don't mind them too much as I do feel regal as I stroll along them surveying my kingdom.

Being on my best behaviour with other dogs, and their pretentious owners, is not up for discussion. Woe-betide if I show my mistress up in public.

So, yes, I do kind of live with a 'Sergeant Major' of sorts; but you must remember that I am always rewarded with treats and they always outweigh my efforts. So, I've decided I'm going to put up with Toni and her silly rules and regulations for the foreseeable future; and for the sake of a pampered lifestyle befitting a king!

Chapter Eight
Aunties, Uncles, Little People and Visitors Bearing Gifts

I have, I know, already mentioned that my Toni is rather a quiet person; she loves her solitary life, her peace and quiet; that is, when I don't set things array. Each morning, she starts the day off in a mild, serene way, however, usually by the end of the day, I have managed to rock her boat, not to mention ruffling her mind, in some way or another and, before you know it, her calm state of equilibrium has vanished and so has my state of tranquillity.

I love her slippers and so does she. I don't care how old and, don't let her see this last word, smelly, they are. In fact, the older and tattier they are, the better, as far as I am concerned. I may have mentioned that she's getting fussy in her 'old age'. This is what I mean; she wears one pair of slippers in the kitchen and changes into another pair once she gets beyond the boundary of the kitchen, into the 'posh' bit of the house. I use the word 'posh' lightly here, for what my mistress regards as 'posh', our present monarch would certainly not. I can only wonder what on Earth she's going to put on her feet if we ever get our modern kitchen. Anyway, if she happens to be in a state of carelessness and leaves her slippers lying around within easy reach, what is a pooch supposed to do? Don't ask me what it is about them; it is certainly not their ghastly smell! Both pairs are as old as the hills and I love them; in fact, I would go so far as to say that I am absolutely obsessed with them. Chewing them is my favourite occupation, but just having them nearby when I go to sleep on a night is a great comfort; especially as they seem to, inexplicably, ease me into delightful dreams of kind aunties, uncles, little people and visitors bearing gifts.

Let's start off with aunties. Well, there's Auntie Anusia, of course; she's my favourite and then there's all of Toni's female friends and acquaintances, who seemed to have adopted me as their honorary nephew, and never fail to bring me a gravy stick, a meaty chew or an interesting toy. Coming back to Auntie Anusia; she's fantastic! She comes armed with treats and I know, with absolute certainty, that she has a soft spot for me. Sometimes, when Toni has a lot on, I end up staying in this relative's house and, but for one blot on the landscape, it's Heaven staying there; my Auntie Anusia spoils me rotten and, more importantly, there are hardly any rules and regulations and definitely no Sergeant Major. The blot on the landscape, to which I am referring, is my cousin, Suzi; a border collie who always looks down on me as an unwelcome intruder. Enough said about Suzi, for the time being; I have honoured her with a chapter of her own.

Uncles are another kettle of fish altogether. I only have one real uncle and he comes with Auntie Anusia. The least said about this particular character, the better; suffice it to say, he is not partial to dogs, even a handsome, intelligent chap like me, but never fear, I have my own way of dealing with him. On the rare occasion he appears on the scene, I bark my head off, staring at him intently as he dares to put one foot forth, then back; his wary eyes on me as his hand attempts to open the gate and then swiftly withdraws. Inwardly, I smile as he nervously digs his hand into his pocket, retrieves the gravy bone in his trembling fingers for all to see, like a visible flag of surrender, he cautiously opens the gate, puts a brave foot forward, his eyes fixated on me and dashes through, hastily throwing the treat in my direction. Now, if he was a clear-thinking man, and we all know he visibly isn't, he could have saved his blood pressure from rising to a dangerous level; all he needed to do was to have given me a treat as soon as he saw me and his safe passage would have been secured. Honestly, there's no teaching some folk, especially as we go through the same ritual during his escape back into the outside world.

I like the little people most of all; I think they call them children. I see them on my walks in the field; from afar they spot me, pointing their fingers in my direction and pulling frustrated mums, dads, grandparents and, anybody else that's with them, towards me.

"It's a bear… it's that lion from that movie… he looks like a fluff ball… he's like a big, round pudding…" All these statements, and others, float towards me; though, I must admit, the last one is a little harsh; as I get patted, stroked, cooed at, admired, given compliments and even hugs. I must say, amidst all this admiration and adulation, I feel very much the king I truly am as I stand there all regal and royal looking, revelling in all the deserved attention. I don't mind if I don't get a treat; just being with these little people makes me feel fantastic.

Before I forget, and race on to another chapter of my life, I must tell you about one incident which, whenever I recall, I can't help but smile. It actually occurred only a couple of weeks ago, when Toni and I were walking along a dusty track in the small field at the back of our house. I felt profoundly contented, my belly full of delicious morsels, as I walked blissfully alongside my mistress, while she was immersed in a pool of her own thoughts.

"Hello Gorgeous," said a low, sexy voice; propelling my mistress and I to snap out of our respective reveries and raise our eyes to the source of the compliment and Toni to stare blatantly at the tall, handsome chap standing before her; in other words, the man of her dreams. You know the kind I mean; the ones you find in fairy tales or locate in soppy movies.

"W-well, t-hank you," she finally stammered and stuttered, her heart all a flutter while I shrivelled inside.

The stranger smiled down at me and switched his eyes to Toni. "Actually, I was talking to the dog."

I watched as the dancing smile died a sudden death on my mistress's lips and, at that instant, I felt I had died along with her smile, for believe it or not, I felt for my owner and wished, at that moment, I could take the embarrassment away from her.

"Oh… I… I know." She attempted a light laugh, but deep inside, I knew she was hurt and I was the cause of it, be it innocently this time. You see, most other gals would have laughed it off, but not my Toni. You see, I knew the embarrassment was not due to the fact that the compliment wasn't intended for her ears; what upset her was the fact that she wrongly jumped to conclusions. As I have mentioned, she is a seriously minded girl and I knew I had a serious job to do that evening.

I set my mind to thinking and there was only one simple solution to it all, I thought, that would ease her tortured soul. That evening as she sat down to read a sizzling bestseller, I retrieved her slipper from its hiding place. I watched as her eyes rose above her thick tome and stared in my direction and, as her hands lowered the book, I could see her mouth set in a disapproving line, as she watched me approaching her with her beloved slipper, firmly gripped between my pearly whites. I could see the red mist covering her eyes; I could sense the tension in her taut body, as I slowly placed one paw in front of the other, my eyes focussed on my mistress, my teeth firmly clenched on my prized possession, my mind set firmly on my important mission. Black thunder, I saw, replaced the hazy mist in her eyes, her mouth growing more mutinous by the second.

"Kameham…" Her mouth remained open, the thunder in her eyes instantly dissipating as I dropped the slipper at her feet and sat by her side, looking as angelic as I possibly could. It worked. I could almost feel the tension in her body evaporating away and her heart melting as she placed her hand on my head; I let her off this time, she'd been through a traumatic time, poor lass. "You are forgiven, Kamehameha." She smiled as she stroked my fur coat. And, that was enough for me. I was in Heaven.

Sorry, I was waylaid there. Going back to unsolicited visitors; unlike my uncle, I do actually look forward to the postman's arrival; for he is indeed a wise bird and always comes armed with a treat. Other official visitors like, for example, the gas, or the electric meter men are always fun to watch; they belong in my uncle's category. Usually, I frighten them half to death with my bark. I, of course, wouldn't hurt them in any way; but, they are ignorant of this fact; so, in the first few seconds of weighing up the problem of entrance, I firmly establish myself as the boss and, for my effort, I am usually rewarded with the ultimate respect I duly deserve. However, the downside of this is that once they get to know me, they tend to ignore my bark and ignore me. So; while they always present me with a treat, attention on me somewhat dwindles. The upside is that when a replacement; or, rather a new victim, comes on the scene, the situation changes and, once again, I have the upper paw. Acquaintances who know me never fail to bring a gift of some sort; so, their passageway is easy; I just let them through without any hassle.

So, all in all, this guarding the house, duty lark, is a breeze and can entail a whole lot of fun. I will say no more on this subject; for, as there is no one in sight, it's time for a well-deserved nap.

Chapter Nine
My Cousin Suzi

My cousin, Suzi. What can I say except that she is an utterly spoilt pooch and that's putting it mildly; it's a wonder I put up with her at all. As you, and Suzi, are well aware I am a descendant, if in name only, from royal Hawaiian stock. Suzi, however, has no regard, or indeed time, for matters of such vital importance. For example, when I arrive on a visit, she barely lifts one eye and when she stops to do so, it's an eye of contemptible distaste. As for moving from her cosy bed, to let me on as a matter of etiquette, as far as she's concerned, I've got no hope. Personally, I think she's jealous; yes, she is jealous of my fantastic good looks and super intelligence. Granted, she's not a bad looking gal herself, as far as border collies go, with her glossy black and white coat, her cute face and sparkling eyes; in fact, I quite fancied her myself at one point, but suffice it to say, she does not have a royal name, therefore, she is a commoner; a mere commoner with an oversized attitude. Now, if it wasn't for her owner, my Auntie Anusia, I wouldn't bother with her at all. So, you see, I have no choice in the matter. I have to put up with Suzi and her gargantuan ego. Such is life!

Anyway, it came to pass one summer, Toni decided to take a trip to her beloved Hawaiian Islands and, instead of forking out some dosh on luxury kennels, she decided to bestow me on my Auntie Anusia, Uncle Mikołaj and cousin Suzi.

I dreaded my mistress's departure, for there was no one like my Toni who I could twist around my paw, as she remained totally oblivious to what was happening. Neither did I relish the prospect of spending two whole weeks: fourteen whole days and nights, in Suzi's company; an hour was as much as I could take, after which I was a successful candidate for the loony bin. And so, during the days leading up to the great upheaval, I spent cunningly plotting ways I could, somehow, entice Suzi on to my side, to make life cushier for myself.

This was not an easy task, for my cousin was well and truly set in her ways and, unlike Toni, I could see she would not bend. It was, therefore, necessary to deploy a number of ingenious plans and put my skills into action. These I have now put forward for your consumption.

Plan One: Sharing

Being the wise 'old' gal she is, Toni had the good sense to buy me some new doggie toys before her departure on the seven seas; so, along with my old toys, and a bagful of doggie treats, I ventured into Suzi's domain. After a lot of thinking, I had decided to get her on my side by allowing her to share my toys. The brute; she not only stared down at them disdainfully; but, to my ultimate shock and horror, demolished them to pieces within minutes of spotting them. So, in the end, I was left with an array of odds and ends, bearing no recognition to their former role as a bone, a sausage or a cat; in fact, as I looked down at the tattered and torn moggy, it served as a poignant reminder of what I should do when; or, rather if, I ever managed to catch one. In utter disgust, I sprawled out on the kitchen floor, with one displeased eye on my cousin, as she wrenched and ripped at the remnants of a colourful ball. What good fun, I thought, Toni and I had with that ball; she throwing it to me and I running, as fast as my legs would allow, retrieving it, bringing it back to my mistress and dropping it at her feet. And now, Toni and the ball were gone.

Sharing my food was the hardest challenge for me to accomplish. I could take or leave food, most of the time; but, to share my food with my cousin, well… You see, Suzi was food mad and would eat everything in sight and what was more infuriating was the fact that, unlike myself, to this very day she has a figure to die for which, I am sure you would agree, is totally unfair. At my residence I enjoy an all-inclusive set up and I partake of meals when, and if, I choose to do so; only, when Suzi comes visiting, I look around and all I'm left with is a shiny, empty bowl; Toni, is of course, delighted that her esteemed guest enjoys the meals she provides and I am always left with one regret, at not having the sense of devouring my meal before Suzi gets her choppers into my chicken flavoured fare.

Auntie Anusia has more sense and she accepts no nonsense of this kind. During my recent stay at her abode, when Suzi was on one of her thieving missions, Auntie Anusia caught her in the act, severely scolded her; a wave of undiluted victory sweeping over me, as my dastardly cousin withdrew from the little food that remained in my dish, curled up in her basket and stared viciously at me. To add fuel to the fire, some hours later, Auntie Anusia presented me with a new toy, her silent, sharp eyes deterring her pet pooch from coming anywhere near me, or my new toy cat; as a final gesture, my cousin turned her back on me and refused to look at me for the duration of the night; so much for my sharing plan.

Plan Two: Living the Solitary Existence

So, as you can see, my first plan did not work at all, in fact, it made matters substantially worse, for Suzi was in the dog house, so to speak, and now wanted absolutely nothing to do with me. So, I quickly got my thinking cap on and came up with a new plan: living a solitary existence. Now, as you know, this could not be accomplished in the strict literary sense of the word, as I was currently residing at my Auntie Anusia's residence with my aunt, uncle and the bane of my life, my cousin, Suzi.

From my past experiences I knew Suzi always craved attention and specifically, Auntie Anusia's attention, so, I decided that during the duration of my visit I would step back and allow Suzi all the attention she demanded because, after all, it was all rightfully hers. Maybe, I foolishly thought, by deploying this route, Suzi and I could, at least, become friends. So, when Auntie Anusia threw tasty delicacies my way, I looked the other way, though, I must say, it took all my doggie willpower to do so. Boy, was it hard! I could smell the delicious beefy and chicken smells; I could almost taste the succulent bits of roast chicken, as saliva involuntarily dribbled out of my hungry mouth. And then… before I knew what I was doing, instinctively I placed one paw in front of the other, my whole body moving towards the chicken piece as my greedy eyes fixated on the golden, crispy skin; soon… soon… it would be in my belly and, just as I was about to make my final move, Suzi came into my line of vision. I stood glued to the floor, my eyes mesmerised… Suzi… chicken… Suzi… chicken… and just as I opened my mouth wide to gobble up the chicken, it disappeared before my very eyes into Suzi's mouth; a satisfied grin lurking around her greedy mouth leaving me to feel empty, in every sense of the word.

Suzi was scolded and sent to her basket, while I was praised, stroked, patted and bestowed with all the attention Auntie Anusia could muster and, when she was done, she lavished on me a selection of tasty treats as she threw a disdainful eye on my disgraced cousin.

Plan Three: Flirting

I was fast running out of plans, but I also knew the best one was yet to materialise; though, I must admit, I was particularly trying to avoid this plan and, most definitely, reserved it only as a last resort when everything else failed. However, here we were, I had arrived at the last resort.

To this day, flirting does not come easy to me; in fact, believe it or not, I have never seriously flirted in my life. You see, as you will readily believe, and agree with me, I have no need to flirt as most female pooches with a grain of sense in their head, will do all the flirting, while I casually assess their potentiality as possible wives; so far, no one has come up to scratch. But, anyway, this time I had a plan. Easy tactics to begin with, I thought, then, if they fail, I would progress on to more advanced, head scratching techniques; I'd worry about those, if I had to, at a later date, I concluded.

So, I began by cautiously approaching Suzi at different times of the day. I would attempt to stroll or run along with her, but she was having none of it as she out walked or out ran me, until I was left well and truly behind; perhaps, I surmised, she thought this to be some sort of strange game.

Tactic number two came into force. I began to gently brush my body against hers and, once, I even placed my paw on her head while she was snoozing. Never again! She turned, snapped and displayed such treacherous teeth; I'm still having repetitive nightmares!

And, so, I had exhausted all my resources; all my plans had failed miserably and, to be honest, I was bored of the whole charade. We went back to our old, familiar ways. Suzi averted her eyes and body away from me and I was relieved not to see her 'mug', as I pretended I wasn't there; in fact, I decided, sulking was the best course of action to take; a bit of self-pity was in order, after all, it was I who was abandoned while my owner went gallivanting halfway across the world without, it seemed, a second thought about me; leaving me to fend for myself and live with that fiend, Suzi, for fourteen whole days and nights. Yes; sulking, I firmly decided, was good and, while I thought about my sorry state, I thought I'd go the whole hog and go on hunger strike too!

I lay on the hard kitchen floor with my nose stuck to the cool tiles, my eyes firmly closed as I stewed in my miserable state, as a series of disturbing and erratic thoughts crashed through my mind. How could Toni just go and leave me, knowing full well I'd suffer in one way or another, while she embarked on the time of her life kayaking, island hopping, swimming in the warm Pacific waters; not to mention visiting sacred sights associated with the Great King Kamehameha, my namesake? And to add to the mix, since she last called Auntie Anusia, there had been scarcely any treats thrown my way; incidentally, I did catch the word 'diet' in that conversation across the waves; so, I had no doubt the Sergeant Major was still, somehow, in control. I only hoped that, in her tropical state of mind, she didn't forget that I was still a growing pooch and I needed to be treated, now and again, to maintain my doggie equilibrium.

Anyway, food came and went, for sadly, my auntie does not run an all-inclusive establishment, if grub wasn't eaten in a certain time, it was simply whisked away and one could only dream about it; so, there I was, dreaming about kabanosy, steaks and other meaty bits and pieces and that's all I did: dream.

I must confess; I was starting to miss home. I missed Toni fussing over me, spoiling me, treating me and, yes, even talking away to me. I know I go on about her prattling away and giving me no peace, when I am in desperate need of a snooze, but now, as I've said, I missed her endless chatter, the background noise of the television, the comforting, lulling sound of Hawaiian guitars, the endless treats, strolling along the stepping stones and I even missed being on kingdom duty; but, most of all, I missed Toni; for, despite Auntie Anusia's best intentions, I was starting to feel like an intruder; an unimportant nobody, though I knew my Auntie Anusia loved the bones off me and I loved her to pieces. I desperately missed being the king of my own castle. So, what started off as being an improvised sulk slowly, and unintentionally, graduated into full scale depression and, before I knew it, I was seriously off food, including treats of any kind, as a heavy blanket of sadness overshadowed me and drew me further into its dark shadows.

It didn't take long for Auntie Anusia to notice something was not quite right, for as I have hinted, she's an observant, wise kind of bird. The distance between Suzi and myself, she dismissed straight away; it was normal and expected. The food business she could understand too, to a certain degree, as Toni had warned her about my erratic eating habits; snubbing my nose at treats, she could not fathom out and this problem deeply perturbed her. The dreaded 'v' word was mentioned. My ears pricked up as I gave a deep, inward sigh. No... no... anything but the dreaded visit to the v—e—t; for, a visit there was never a delightful experience; a fate worse than death itself. So, now it seemed, there was a looming possibility of a doggie doctor probing me about and issuing me with some foul-tasting pills, Auntie Anusia would surely try to disguise, in the form of tasty cookies, or, bits of irresistible chocolate; only, I've gone off treats, so I wondered how she would get around that specific dilemma. Consequently, we were not having a great time; except, that is, apart from Suzi. She seemed to take pleasure in my misery as she made a point of snuggling up close to Auntie Anusia, eating all the food put in front of her, though that's nothing new, and uncharacteristically being good.

I felt all alone in the big, wide world and the v— e— t was hovering; all because my plan went into orbit and showered me with problems I did not foresee, and all this, because my cousin, Suzi, failed to recognise me as someone important. However, I couldn't help considering that, if it wasn't for my silly plans, I wouldn't be in this mess at all; so, I set to thinking once again. What could I do? I certainly didn't want that dastardly v—e—t on the scene; or, anywhere within a hundred-kilometre radius and even that would be too near for my comfort. With my thinking cap firmly on, I thought hard and furiously; for, speed, I knew, was of the essence.

The bowl of food came out at its customary time and I could see, and smell, the tasty bits of kabanos and fresh roast chicken placed in the dish as an extra form of enticement. I sniffed a little deeper… deeper still, as I began to feel the familiar rise of saliva trying to escape. I rose and cautiously crept to the carefully prepared feast. For a brief few seconds I stared at the food, for giving in to temptation was not the way of a king. I closed my eyes to obliterate the lure of scrumptious chicken pieces; only, for the v… e… t to appear, as large as life, a packet of something awful in his hand. Quickly, I opened my eyes and, without a second thought, devoured everything in the bowl and, after my self-induced famine, what a banquet it was! And, the praise and adulation I received from Auntie Anusia was an extra bonus.

At this point of the proceedings, Suzi, from her vantage point, had cocked her head in readiness for her share of rewards, witnessing only more bits of kabanos being thrown into my empty bowl. Begrudgingly, she rose and stealthily took steps towards me, belying the rush of doggie anger sweeping through her body like a wild tsunami, for she had seen with her own eyes what, she thought, was a betrayal of the gravest concern.

Auntie Anusia had inadvertently saved the day by temporarily switching her allegiance, and attention, to me and, in the process; at long last, I had won Suzi's attention. I deemed it wise to allow by cousin to stand by my side, feeling her nudge ever closer as I felt her soft fur against my body. I didn't revel in her intimacy too much, as I spied another tasty morsel in my bowl; hastily, I devoured it before my greedy cousin got her teeth into the juicy meat.

That evening, I did give her my permission to share my food and together we ate; an experience in history which was never to be repeated. To everyone's utter surprise, we ended up spending the night together on my king size duvet; but, by early morning Suzi had left my bed and, to be honest with you, I was mighty thankful, for when I had embarked on my zealous flirtations, little did I realise that for one to have a girlfriend, one had to share one's food, bed, toys and treats. It was, let me tell you, a stark lesson to digest, and one I shall never forget, as I continue to enjoy my solitary existence. As for a future potential wife; forget it!

Chapter Ten
Walkies, Delightful
Interruptions and Tantrums

Ever since I could walk, the sight of a lead would make my heart pound with excitement and joy. I was ready to go anywhere, everywhere and at any time; short distances, long distances, to the end of the world would have suited me well; through rough terrain or smooth, I didn't care as long as I was on the move. So, it was a delight, and an added bonus, to realise that Toni was herself health conscious; though, far from successful most of the time, when it comes to a strict exercise regime; but, bless her, she's a trier.

At first there was, as I have mentioned, just the garden, where I scampered up and down the stepping stones to my heart's delight. Later, we ventured out on short walks around the block and, later still, we made for the wide-open freedom of the fields. However, although I was excited by the sight of a lead, as it inevitably signalled a stroll of some sort, I passionately hated the feel and constraint it brought with it and, on many occasions, I tried to furtively make a bid for freedom. Being the know-all she is, Toni, I knew, suspected my plan; the tugs, twists and turns, I assumed, gave her a clue. In response, she gripped the lead tighter, pulling me closer to her-self and I felt well and truly trapped, my freedom diminishing by the second. Don't get me wrong I loved walking along with my mistress, receiving bountiful compliments on my good looks from all and sundry; but, I yearned, at the same time, to break free.

I was about three years of age at the time. I remember it was a hot, oppressive day, during mid-August, as Toni and I were leisurely strolling side by side, along the bottom of the woods. It was a real joy to watch the rabbits hop about, without a care in the world; how I envied their freedom. For some unknown reason, I raised my eyes to Toni and noticed that her attention was not fully on me, which, obviously, was not too good when she had a pooch of such regal status strolling by her side. I let it go, knowing by her glazed look that she was probably reminiscing of her long-ago childhood: climbing trees, making dens, collecting cones and wild flowers; she was well and truly lost in those happy, bygone days. I also noticed the tension had become loose on my lead. Again, I raised my eyes to my mistress, but she was hiding behind ancient trees, or collecting brambles. Yes, she was lost in time; and, this was my time to make my own memories. My eyes now switched, and focussed, on my destination. I gave one firm, unexpected tug and away I fled as fast as my legs would carry me. Briefly, I looked around to witness an astounded Toni, who had so rudely been thrust out of her pleasurable memories, back to the present time, looking around her in a state of bewilderment. This was no time to start feeling sorry for her; quickly, I gathered speed, my grit and determination aiding me greatly as I sped like the wind.

"Kamehameha… Kamehameha… come back…" I heard her call frantically somewhere in the distance, but, this pooch was not for turning. Vague memories of an adventurous Bonfire Night, a couple of years ago, crashed into my thoughts; I hastily dismissed them as I ran faster and faster, past other dogs and their owners, past the tennis courts and the bowling club at the end of the field; onward and forward I ploughed, a rush of exhilarating freedom surging through every quick pulsating vein in my body. Eventually, I decreased my speed, turned and, to my horror, Toni was nowhere to be seen; not even a bleak speck on the horizon; I was alone in the vast field. There was no point running anymore, I decided, and, anyway, it would be a good idea to conserve my energy for future use, I concluded, as I strolled along the curvy path at the far end of the field.

Meanwhile, Toni had gone into the woods, calling after me, searching around every Ash, Elm and Oak and then into the nearby neighbourhood scanning the roads, snickets and gardens; asking anyone and everyone for any clues concerning my whereabouts.

She'd been gone for what seemed like hours and then I heard the clanking of the gate. I must admit, I'd already enjoyed a long, cool drink of water and a good hour's snooze by then. Slowly, I raised my eyes, perched primly against the back door, extended my paw and awaited my fate.

As I chewed on the marrowbone pieces, I could feel the sense of relief sweeping over Toni. "What a clever pooch I have." She sighed as my brain whirled, planning my next escape into the great outdoors.

I know that I have briefly mentioned that grooming is a no-no word; it is, actually, far worse than that. It is the worst thing I can possibly think of, and I avoid it all costs. In fact, it does not deserve another mention, and I'm certainly not going to waste a chapter on this horrible subject, as I have far more delightful topics to think about. I am only going to say that because of my non-conformity regarding any form of grooming paraphernalia, I have ended up sprucing myself up. You see, due to my royal status, I cannot possibly go out into the world, meeting my subjects, looking like a tramp. Now, on these long walks that Toni and I enjoy, I pick up all kinds of interesting objects that annoyingly get entangled and stuck in my long, beautiful fur. This is very frustrating, to say the least, because I just haven't got the patience; or, the inclination, to stand there while Toni painstakingly searches through, what seems like, every strand of fur to disentangle the offending alien. Can you imagine, standing still like a pin, while she diligently picks, then pokes, pulls and, dare I say, tears at my coat as if I was some sort of chicken being prepared for the roasting platter, until she finally manages to extract a cone that has seen better days; or, a thistle; more often than not, a host of dead bits of leaves or twiglets? I would be only too glad to save her the bother; for, I hate these unsolicited bits and pieces decorating me, as if I was some kind of exotic Christmas tree; and, if she'd only employ a gram of patience and understanding of the situation, and bide her time, she would see that I would see to the business myself with, I hasten to add, a fraction of the fuss and effort she applies. For, on occasion, when Toni is unable to sort me out, I sort myself out with a technique that will probably make your hair curl with amazement. I undertake this job at a leisurely pace; but, with the utmost seriousness because my great looks are at stake. First, I sit myself down in a comfortable spot, normally on the kitchen floor or on one of the stepping stones in the garden; I locate the twiglet, thistle or leaf and examine whether I need to proceed with the process of easing the alien out with the aid of my pearly whites, or simply leaving it until it decides to vacate my premises on its own accord. And that's all there is to it; business is done. I have, on several occasions, tried to show Toni my unique skills by attempting to solve the problem myself, in the midst of our stroll, but she was having none of it. Oh no, she has to stick her nose in and make the business her problem. To this day, I haven't decided whether she's on to the job for the sake of my appearance and, more importantly her pride; or, my comfort. The thing is, I fear this issue shall never be resolved; the lure of the bramble bush, the colourful crackling autumnal leaves, or simply walking where I want to, without a care in the world is too much for me to resist, even though my mistress does keep me on a tight leash most of the time.

Tantrums; now, here's a word that doesn't seem to register in Toni's vocabulary; though, I must admit, personally I'm quite susceptible to a good old tantrum, now and again; especially when things go awry and are not going my way. This sometimes happens when I'm in the mood for a little bit of socialising, with other pooches of the same inkling, who seem only too willing to oblige; though Toni, at the time, is not willing at all. She pulls me away, smiles at the owner of my potential friend and drags me on. She gets her comeuppance when I decide to sit in the middle of the field, or pavement, and refuse to move. At that point, wild horses won't entice me to move a centimetre; especially if I firmly choose not to budge. I just sit on my hind legs, looking pretty and highly intelligent, to the delight of other dog owners who, incidentally, find this performance fantastically amusing. Toni, I must say, does not, as she drags and scolds; threatens me with treat bans; but, as I have mentioned, nothing on Earth will make me move unless I want, and choose, to move. In these scenarios, I always get my way, as she makes the ultimate mistake of pretending to walk off in another direction and, in that instance, I make a bid for freedom and, eventually, make my own way home usually arriving and sitting sedately at the back door, long before my frazzled owner makes an appearance.

And so, there you have it. Walks are always a pleasure, one way or another and I love them!

Chapter Eleven
Holiday Time and
Hawaiian Madness

I look forward to the annual holiday with a bunch of mixed feelings. Actually, in fact, I don't get a holiday as such; usually I end up in my Auntie Anusia's house; though, on one occasion, I spent my annual vacation in a place called the 'kennels'. In my eight years of residing on this planet, I have only once been a guest at these kennels and once was enough, thank you very much. Heavenly Homes Kennels was, I must admit, a very nice place; each guest had his, or her, allocated space with blankets, toys and other doggie accessories brought from home; we were fed well, taken for regular walks, fussed over by employees and passing visitors and even the socialising between the inmates was a pleasant experience; but, I much prefer the peace and solitude of my own kingdom; where Toni is at my beck and call and I am the only one, rather than one of many.

As I recall, immediately as I walked into the spacious grounds of Heavenly Homes Kennels, my senses were alive to the sudden change of smell and noise volume and wondered how this would affect my peace of mind. I walked, with my proud head held high, past the other pooches in their pens; for, I am a great believer of first impressions and if I was to attain, and maintain, my sovereign status, I had to play the appropriate role perfectly. To my almost immediate and utter dismay, I quickly realised that everyone here was equal and no one was treated differently; a thing I knew I had to get used to and accept if I was to have any quality of life here at all. Within minutes of my arrival, I was escorted to my personal pen with a yapping, gorgeous looking white Poodle situated on one side of me and a vicious looking Alsatian on the other; while I, the great Kamehameha, was stuck in the middle of these two specimens. My first reaction was to focus my eyes directly ahead and totally ignore them both and to get as comfortable as I possibly could get, in this state-of-the-art prison for pooches;

for, let's face it, we had all been temporarily abandoned through no fault of our own.

On my arrival and her imminent departure, Toni fussed over me like some mother hen, warning me to be a good boy, encouraging me to behave, promising me the world on a golden platter on her return, telling me she wanted to hear 'good stories' about me. I switched off. I didn't want to come here in the first place and, now that I was stuck here, I wish she'd just turn away and disappear and leave me to my fate, as her lingering was breaking my heart in two.

I can't tell you much about that particular evening, as I simply curled up in a furry ball on my plush duvet, closed my eyes and pretended to be asleep, with the sound of constant yapping, and an infuriating variety of high- and low-pitched barking, filling my senses. Finally, I managed to, somehow, close my mind to it all and fall into a deep slumber.

As the days rolled by, my initial theory was realised; for I came to understand with clear clarity, that I would never rise to achieving the status of sovereign in this compound; but, I had already established myself as nothing less than an equal. The gorgeous Poodle I found, to my annoyance, was too much like my cousin, Suzi, for my liking; and one Suzi was enough for me in this lifetime and the next. However, the Alsatian became a sturdy friend. Whenever we were let loose, we would romp around, run and play together and I quickly learned that first impressions were not always what they seemed.

Now, I am not a stupid pooch as I am sure, by now, you have realised. No way was I going to allow Toni to think that Heavenly Home Kennels was 'Heaven' in name and 'Heavenly' in nature; for if, even for a moment, she thought I was having a great time, she would stick me in here at the drop of a hat. I needn't have worried my head over the matter; for, by the time Toni came to collect me, the playful Alsatian and the stuck-up, self-obsessed Poodle had flown the nest, so to speak; so, when my mistress entered the vicinity, she spotted a forlorn, lonely Kamehameha, huddled in a ball in the corner of a solitary 'cell'. I must admit, I felt a bit of a fraud as I acted out brilliantly the role of a forsaken pooch; why, even that gal I resemble, who stars in those movies, would have been proud of my Oscar winning performance; but needs must, as they say.

"Oh Kamehameha… Kamehameha… are you all right? I am here… you're coming home… Oh Kamehameha, my little treasure… I'll never leave you again… never…" My ears pricked up. Was that a good or a bad thing? I seriously wondered.

Hawaiian madness, that's what I call Toni's crazy behaviour. Not only was I named after the Great King Kamehameha of Hawaii; but now, she has taken into slotting Hawaiian words and phrases into our daily conversation. I mean, how ludicrous is that? More and more I think she belongs in a loony bin and even there, I think, they would scratch their heads in puzzlement. She began with Aloha which, I guess, was quite harmless enough; after all, who isn't influenced in some way, by their time spent in a foreign country; especially if they have a strong bond with the place? Aloha, if you are struggling to grasp the meaning means hello, goodbye and I love you. Now, if it was just that greeting of a morning; or, perhaps last thing at night, I could live with it; but, her sentences have become more and more sprinkled with the Hawaiian lingo. In fact, it was my misfortune that she treated herself to a Hawaiian phrase book. As soon as I spotted the thing, I knew it spelt trouble and I was proved right. The following words were soon firmly fixed into her vocabulary: mahalo – thank you, noho – sit, wawae aku – paw, and these were only for starters; many more followed and remained. And that's how I became a pooch versed in three languages: English, Polish and Hawaiian.

The lilting sounds of Hawaiian music suited my personality perfectly; for, as you know, I am, generally speaking, serene and even tempered and the soft, calming strumming of the ukuleles and Hawaiian guitars do my spirit good; though, I'm not too sure what our neighbour, Mister Frobisher, thinks of Hawaiian melodies constantly floating through his open windows.

Traditional Hawaiian recipes; however, are not to my liking. I'm still not sure whether Toni's Hawaiian Haupia pudding should taste as it does; whether she just can't bake; or, whether she's laboriously trying to poison me. Anyway, I sampled this coconut milk based square and the long and short of it is; I sample it never again, if I want to live.

I will now embark on describing to you the Hawaiian evening she had planned, long before she ever set off on her hols to tropical climes. Of course, needless to say, on her return, everything was Hawaiian. Each day, Toni would wear a different Hawaiian print dress, blouse, top, leggings or trousers and imitation Hawaiian gods were dotted around the house. Thank goodness our Parish Priest was not on the warpath, for these gods do not align well with the spirit of Catholicism; they looked grotesque and scared me half to death. Hawaiian music played throughout the school holidays and I, of course, was unfortunately the chief sampler of her traditional Hawaiian cakes and pastries, in preparation of this great, long-awaited evening. It was to take place on a Saturday and a selection of Toni's honoured friends, Auntie Anusia and Uncle Mikołaj, thankfully not Suzi, were invited. My intention was to surreptitiously slope off into a corner and have a good, old nap. Well, that's what I thought. Toni, on the other hand, had other ideas.

For a few evenings, I had seen her engaged in creating something out of colourful card, tissue paper, silk flowers, foliage and colourful exotic material. Never, in a million years, would I have guessed her desired intention. At the side entrance to the front door, she had assembled a cave-like structure, over which was placed a hibiscus decorated drape, leaving a large opening at the front. Inside this cave was a seat, resembling a throne. Don't ask me how she created this rather beautiful looking edifice; it's too complicated to describe, even for a super intelligent pooch like me. Suffice it to say it was covered with colourful, silk orchids, plumeria, oleander, lehua blossoms and even a silver-sword thrown in for good measure and all the tropical flora was interwoven with a delightful array of foliage. I stood transfixed, my eyes mesmerised by the sight before me and then, I saw it… my astonished eyes stuck to the label above. I stared and stared, my incredulous eyes almost popping out of their sockets as I slowly read the words: KAMEHAMEHA WELCOMES YOU. ALOHA! And there, I guessed, I was to sit, meet and greet our esteemed guests. If only that was the end of it! Carefully, Toni placed around my neck, lei after colourful lei, until I felt myself drowning in a sea of colourful, tickly leis. My duty, I guessed correctly, was to meet and greet our guests in true traditional Hawaiian style.

The soft lilting music was turned on seductively low, I was sat on my throne and Toni, in her blue Hawaiian print dress and an artificial hibiscus, of her own creation, in her hair, was waiting expectantly for our honoured guests to arrive. They came dressed in tropical attire and, on their entrance, Toni extracted a lei from my overloaded neck, and placed it over their heads; thus, relieving me of my uncomfortable flowery burden; but, not only that, I had been trained to present my paw in time with every Aloha greeting. The rest of the evening, I am glad to say, went by in a total blur.

I would have gladly placed the Hawaiian evening into the far recesses of my mind, to be buried and forgotten. This was not to be. Every day, as I walk past the numerous framed photographs, I am reminded of that ghastly evening and, lest I should forget, Toni never fails to greet me every morning with a lively, heartfelt "Aloha, Kamehameha!"

Chapter Twelve
Renovations, Unexpected Interruptions and Opportunities

For years and years, as far back as my intelligent mind will take me, Toni had been rabbiting on about kitchen renovations; years came and went and we still had the same old, poky, dark and certainly, out of date, kitchen; well, at least, that's how she described it. It surely did not fit in well with the rest of our modern house and, of course, it would be the place where I normally reside. I mean, have you ever heard of a king being banished from entering the rooms of his own castle? Yet, here I am, in the servant's quarters, on the outside, looking in. My namesake, the Great King Kamehameha of Hawaii is, no doubt, looking down in total disgust and would probably have my mistress's head on a spike if he could possibly get to her! So, here I am, a king in the scullery and, let me tell you, I am none too pleased; it's a very dismal situation indeed.

It's her own fault that we are stuck with this distasteful carbuncle. If she'd had more common sense than money, instead of gallivanting back and forth to Hawaii at every conceivable opportunity like some out of control yo-yo, we would be on our third, or even fourth, kitchen by now. Instead, we both have to suffer the consequences and there are many.

First of all, as I have mentioned, the so-called kitchen is poky, dark and totally unwelcoming and, to add to my misery, I have to sleep in this miserable place because, for love or money, she will not allow me to sleep in her lounge ever since I had my little accident. So you can imagine, if it wasn't for my ability to escape into a snooze at the drop of a hat and dream of succulent sausages or capturing the neighbour's cat, the nights would be very long and utterly unbearable.

When both of us are occupying the kitchen at the same time, you can imagine how it is. We have kind of learned to manoeuvre our way around each other, in order to get to our desired spot; but woe-betide her if she accidentally treads on my paw!

Home baking is another sore point. She won't do any claiming, to all and sundry, the oven is not reliable; she hasn't got the right ambience, whatever that is; so, consequently, I miss out on tasty dishes like steak and kidney pudding, sausage rolls, apple pie; or even a chocolate muffin, or two; so, you can't blame me for feeling rather deprived and short-changed.

If I was a visiting health and safety officer, not that one of those would want to enter this danger zone; I would enforce restraining restrictions on this breakneck area of our home. Let me tell you, I have nearly broken my neck, and one of my legs, a number of times. First, there is the loose ceramic tile on the floor on which I continuously manage to catch my paw, but, worse still, is the step leading from the kitchen to the back porch which, in turn, leads into the toilet and pantry. I say pantry; I understand it used to be used as a coalhouse in pre-historic days; now, anything goes in there: tins of food, pots and pans, shoes, boots, brooms and dusters and, most annoyingly, my food, blankets and treats! Anyway, this step has caused many accidents. I have rushed out on my eager way to the back garden, only to end up sprawling over it; Toni has left behind a pedicured red polished toe nail and, in the days when visitors were allowed into this area many, unfortunately, had not realised the cursed step was there until it was too late.

We don't have a breath-taking view from our present kitchen window, only a tall fence and the sky above and when I bird watch, which I love to do. Toni moves me on for sitting and staring too long and barking with joy when I happen to spot one of my feathered friends and, more importantly, for being in her way. For goodness' sake, how is an intelligent pooch supposed to fill his time? So, yes, we are due for a new, modern kitchen and, I am glad to say, plans are beginning to formulate.

At first, strangers came and went; some with long tapes stretching up, down and across our poky kitchen, pens scribbled on bits of paper, heads were scratched and then nothing happened for a long while. Toni continued to go to work; I continued to be on bird duty and all remained status quo. Then, Toni stopped going to work and things began to happen. More strangers arrived on the scene, a wall was knocked down, the roof was raised, a thing called a girder was fitted into place, and a temporary tarpaulin spread over the roof; now, that seemed okay because the weather was on our side and we were enjoying an extended spell of hot weather. Anyway, that evening, Toni had taken herself off to a church service and I was left amongst the debris, rubble and chaos, to be the sole guardian of the house. I must say, I was feeling pretty lonely and miserable because, although the builders had cleared up before leaving, it was still a dark, dusty and gloomy place. However, my state of mind was nothing to what I was going to experience later that evening.

In my dismal state, I must have, somehow, dozed off; for, the pitter-patter of raindrops against the window stirred me from a rather nice dream. To my further dismay, as my sleepy eyes gazed around and upwards, I noticed that the rain was coming through an open, flapping gap of the tarpaulin and missing my back by mere centimetres. I watched, mesmerised, as the drops fell in a regular rhythm on to the floor; the drops, I observed, were becoming larger and were creating a puddle in a dip in the floor; eventually, the large puddle begin to overflow the dip and spread across the floor. The rain and wind, by now, were pounding and thrashing mercilessly against the tarpaulin and, as I flicked my eyes to the window, I noticed black clouds had gathered overhead and the rain was lashing down in straight rods. My whole body quivered uncontrollably, my eyes alerted to a sudden flash of light, followed by a horrific growling sound; could this be the end of poor me? Was I going to be gobbled up by some kind of treacherous, ravenous monster? Quick, as the lightning overhead, I snapped out of my dismal predicament. This was no time to start feeling sorry for myself. My eyes darted back to the dip, which had now totally disappeared, the water on its onward march towards the hall door. Disaster! Toni would go ballistic if her precious carpets were ruined; I'd never hear the end of it and this impending catastrophe was surely going to take place if something, or someone, didn't intervene. Kamehameha, to the rescue!

As you know, I am all for creature comforts; but, needs must; so, after surveying the situation with my critical eye, reluctantly, I rose and placed myself against the door leading to the hall and the precious carpets and I pressed myself against the hard wood and glass. Looking back on it all, I can honestly say this was one of the worst evenings I have ever had the misfortune to experience, for not only was the cold water slowly spreading towards me, and surrounding me on all three sides, it was rising. I better not exaggerate if I have plans on entering doggie Heaven; it was not rising fast, more like a snail's pace, but nevertheless, it was rising and I did not like the look of it at all. By now my limbs were starting to feel the cold and stiffness was beginning to creep in, but I dared not move a muscle for fear of the water seeping through into the hall. I weighed up the situation very carefully in my super intelligent head. I could, of course, move away at any time, find a more comfortable spot, possibly get back to that lovely dream and Toni would be none the wiser of me deserting my post; she'd think I had been snoozing, like any sensible dog would, and missed the disaster, or, worse still, she would come to the conclusion that my intelligence didn't stretch to cover such situations. No, I would have to grin and bear it if I was to be any hero at all and, what a hero I'd be if I ended up saving the day! Potential scenarios flashed vividly through my mind: a lifetime of unlimited delicious treats, probably a bigger piece of roast chicken on a Sunday, thick cuts of steak, an endless supply of kabanosy, cakes, chocolate, cookies; the list was never ending, most delightful and determined my immediate fate. There was no way I was going to desert my post with such rewards staring me in my face; so, like a true, honourable and brave soldier, I forgot about an AWOL, as my eyes stared glumly at the water surrounding me.

She must have been praying for England, for her departure seemed eons ago and the rain was still lashing down quickly and furiously, with the odd burst of lightning and clap of thunder added to the dastardly mix. Oh, how I wished she would come home; if only to relieve me of my gruelling duty. My tired eyes rose to the gap in the roof, my ears now accustomed to the frantic thrashing and flapping of the tarpaulin in the angry wind, creating a wider gap, thus allowing more rain in to add to my sorry state. I pressed my body further towards the door for fear of the water seeping through the threshold; pressing further and further into the wood; it was, after all, my duty. Let's see, I thought, if she ever dares to joke about my being on duty again after this episode!

I must have dozed off, for when I opened my eyes, there was Toni standing over me, an umbrella in her hand, smiling down at me. If she thinks this is amusing, I concluded, she is seriously warped in the head.

"Oh, Kamehameha… Kamehameha… you have saved the day!" She exclaimed as she cast her eyes around. "You are absolutely great… the Great Kamehameha!" She laughed as she buried her head in my wet coat. This was praise indeed and I knew that, when we were finally enjoying our new kitchen, neither of us would ever forget this episode.

Chapter Thirteen
Reflecting on the Joys
of the Seasons

Such is the flow of life: day follows day and transcends into weeks, the weeks into months and, before you know it, another year has passed us by. If you were to ask me to choose my favourite season, I would be stuck for an answer as I truly love each one equally; feeling each season brings with it a good measure of happiness, intermingled with a tinge of sadness at its passing.

Although most of the time I like to live in the moment; grab each opportunity and make the most of it, I do like to reflect on the past from time to time and have slipped into a state of melancholy once or twice. I firmly agree with the saying that life is a rich tapestry full of happiness, sadness and every other emotion interwoven into these two strong emotions; sprinkled generously with laughter, tears, expectancy, hope, broken dreams, ambitions and a certain amount of having to accept one's fate; although, I must say, the last challenge, I feel, is sometimes a little hard to take, especially if it doesn't comply with one's plans.

Spring

Let's start with this delightful season, which I very much look forward to, mainly because I can get away from under Toni's feet and do my own thing outside. The weather, of course, becomes warmer; but, not too hot that I am jumping out of my skin. This particular season never fails to bring with it a sense of curiosity and an inexplicable urge to go exploring; though, this can often lead me into all kinds of mischief and trouble of one sort or another.

I have a soft spot for spring flowers; not only are they clothed in the most vivid and splendid colours of orange, yellow, red and white to name but a few; when I stick my nose into their fragrant petals, they give off the most heady and divine scent. No matter how many springs I have lived through, spring flowers are always a source of wonder for an inquisitive nose like mine. Take, for example, the snowdrop. I saw my first snowdrop in my first winter of life. In fact, I almost missed them altogether, for snow lay hard and fast on the ground and it was difficult to spot their snowy white overcoats, even for an observant guy like me. I came across these delightful specimens as I was taking a brisk, solitary stroll along the stepping stones. Cautiously, I approached them, suspicion tingling through every vein in my body. Were they edible? If they were edible, were they tasty? Would they bite; or, run away from me if I touched them with my paw? Slowly, as I put one foot in front of the other, and when I was almost upon them I stopped, my eyes entranced by their bell-like shape. I nudged my nose closer feeling a little disappointed because I could smell nothing. Intrigued, I sat on the cold, soft snow and touched one with my paw and watched, as if bewitched, as it swung delectably from side to side. I touched it again… and again, and wondered at their simple beauty; their delicacy and uniqueness. Just like me, I thought, one of a kind.

Crocuses, what colourful delights of nature: white, orange, lavender and purple; each one innocent and beautiful in its simple design. How carefully formed, I thought, as with my astute eyes, I examined their grass-like leaves, with white stripes along the middle and their colourful cup shaped flowers.

My long nose is particularly drawn to the strong, heady scent of the hyacinth, with its narrow, long leaves and purple, cream, pink flowers. There is nothing better than to sit, or lay, by a cluster of hyacinths and drink in their heavenly perfume.

Tulips are a must with me and, I'm sure you'll agree, they are so beautiful in their simplicity. Again, I like to stick my nose into their cup or star formed flowers of maroon, black, purple, white, cream, yellow, red and pink.

Daffodils are always a pleasure to behold and savour, for they are bright and sunny looking and never fail to cheer me up. So, as you can see, I simply adore all kinds of spring flowers.

Birds are pleasant creatures to watch as they fly gracefully by; but in the spring, they can also be a curse; for, there is nothing worse in this world than being involuntarily serenaded at the crack of dawn, when one is in the midst of dreaming about sausages, roast chicken or huge slabs of mouth-watering chocolate.

Also, for reasons I cannot explain, I cannot abide my two-legged feathered friends whizzing past the kitchen window. When one does happen to cross my line of vision I bark, twirl around in circles, stare and make such strange noises, the v— e—t would be very interested in researching. This kind of chaotic behaviour automatically propels Toni's instant appearance and, let's just say, the kitchen becomes a hubbub of shouting, barking, twirling, stepping on each other's toes, nipping, screaming until all spirals out of control and descends into a state of complete mayhem and the innocent bird has flown merrily by. So, yes I love birds; but, in their proper places, namely their nests.

Summer

Summer allows me to enjoy long, blissful days in the sunshine where there is always the potential to experience new adventures. Normally, I spend the long days in the shade, snoozing, whenever I can get away with it; preferably in the shade somewhere where I can inhale the sweet smell of lilac and jasmine; or, the fragrance of some flowery conditioner as Toni's washing flaps happily on the line. Now, don't get me started on washing lines; or, rather the laundry that goes on them; to this very day I have flashbacks of Toni's oversized pants on Mister Frobisher's pole!

In the summer months, we generally venture on longer walks and, of course, female pooches generally look more spruced up, more attractive and appealing in my discerning eyes; some even have ribbons and bows in their coats which, quite honestly, I'd love to get my paws on, given half the chance.

At this time of the year, Toni eagerly embarks on her gardening and, even though the garden, with its grasses and shrubs, is low maintenance, she doesn't let a day go by without a routine inspection. Personally, I feel that this is some kind of obsession, for if she finds three weeds, she's on a lucky streak. I follow her on her daily rounds; perhaps, I'm becoming obsessed too!

Water and summer go together; ask any of the little people and they will tell you the same thing. Anyway, it was my sixth summer when Toni decided to join Auntie Anusia and cousin Suzi, and allowed me to tag along with them to a beauty spot, about an hour's drive away. All went according to plan. The four of us had enjoyed a relaxing day: Toni and Auntie Anusia reading; or, more often than not, gossiping which, as you know, is their favourite pastime; Suzi and I snoozed away and ignored each other. Purely out of chance, at the end of what seemed like a perfect summer's day, Suzi and I uncharacteristically, and to both our amazements, joined forces against the enemy.

I was in the midst of a glorious dream; a string of fat, juicy sausages hanging enticingly before me and as I eagerly stretched my paw to retrieve them, I opened my eyes to a large, unfriendly looking ginger and white cat. My eyes stretched wider, my paw further as the rude moggy, without a care in the world, unashamedly eyeballed me and, may I hasten to add, not a strand of his fur was standing on end, not even an arched back in evidence. There it was, before my saucer-like eyes; the thought of becoming my supper never entering its silly head. What was I to do? Instinct dictated the matter; for, while the feline seemed perfectly calm and unruffled, and, maybe because of this factor, I felt a surge of boiling blood rush through every vein in my body. The audacity of this stupid creature, who clearly had no intention of running for his life; who was, in fact, perfectly at ease in my company, while my heart pounded; thunderous anger overtaking all my senses and, before I knew what was happening, I sprang and made a leap for him. The moggy, by now, was beginning to have second thoughts about me, for he suddenly turned and ran as fast as his little legs would carry him. I ran. Suzi, opening her eyes to the sudden commotion, decided she didn't want to be left out of the proceedings and joined in giving chase. We whizzed past shocked onlookers packing bags and blankets into boots of cars; trees, bushes, mothers with prams; past a paddling pool and a family of waddling ducks on their way to the pond; so fast we ran, I could only see a spurge of ginger and white in front. I didn't know where I was going, neither did I care. Somewhere in the far distance I heard Toni's familiar voice; but everyone, including herself, knew it was a futile cry on her part. I had one solitary goal in mind and that was to capture my prey. What I was going to do with it once it was caught, for the tabby's sake; I didn't wish to contemplate at that time. By now, other dogs had inspected the situation from their different vantage points, thought it looked like good fun, and decided to join in much to the gasp, horror, cheers and complete joy of the onlookers. There's no denying the cat had speed and, I guess, had outran a great deal of pooches in his time. As for me, my energy was quickly ebbing away; my resolve was weakening; the distance between my victim and I was growing larger by the second and victory was diminishing before my very eyes. Just before I was about to give up, I spotted the cat paddling at the edge of the lake. My energy miraculously recharged, I made a dash for the infuriating moggy. Faster and faster my legs sped, with Suzi and my other loyal followers in my wake. Into the lake I scrambled, going I knew not where, as my victim became ever more elusive. Deeper and further; further and deeper I waded, sure I would spot the unfortunate tabby any moment. As if hypnotised by a force unknown, I swam further and, before I knew it, I was surrounded on all sides by the cool, deep feel of the lapping water all around me. I was alone. No cat; no Suzi and where had all my fans gone? The only consolation to it all was the cooling process and, in minutes, I felt suitably refreshed, ready to exit the lake and make my way back to my mistress. However, I soon realised it was not going to be as easy as I had casually presumed. I turned, homeward bound; only, to my utter dismay, as I attempted to doggie paddle my way out, I found I couldn't. Exerting more strength, I achieved nothing; I was going nowhere. My foot was stuck in something long and snake-like and the more I pushed, tugged and wriggled, trying to free myself, the more my captured foot became entangled in the long stuff. Dismally, I concluded, I was well and truly stuck, and no one was rushing to my aid; in fact, there was no living thing in sight, except for a couple of sticklebacks, with whom I couldn't be bothered to pass the time of day. I had, after all, a much more pressing issue to solve. I tugged harder at the elongated, stringy thing, whatever it was; but, it was no use; yelping and whining didn't get me anywhere either except for plunging me further into a deeper state of irritation and frustration. Surely, I thought, someone will come to my rescue soon; Toni, by now, must be panicking. I scanned my eyes around the immediate periphery. How could they all just abandon me and leave me to my fate. There was nothing else to do but to open my mouth and bark continuously with all of my might and… wait.

As dusk fell, the ferocity of my barking increased, and all I could hear was the sound of my own voice. Any resolve I had was now dwindling away and, I knew I was not living up to my namesake, the Great Kamehameha of Hawaii. How swiftly the great and the good fall. Now, all there was left to do was to start preparing myself for a watery grave, but what was heart wrenching was the fact that no one would ever know what became of me. Such is life; or indeed, the end of it.

And so it is, when one is approaching the end; reflections of one's past come sharply into focus: the happy and sad times; the good and the bad; the lowlights and the highlights; I considered them all as I tried to psyche myself up to meet my Maker. All things considered, I came to the conclusion that I am, or rather, was, a pretty good pooch; though I'm sure Toni would have one or two things to say on that point. I thought my Maker would agree with me that I have been rather an upstanding sort of pooch. I cared for Toni and, unbeknown to her, I was very loyal, for if her life had ever been in danger, I would willingly have paid for it with my own, which is more than I can say for her loyalty. I was a good guard dog and obeyed some of the rules some of the time. My downfall was treats and the lengths I'd go to secure them. I blame my mistress for my weakness, for if she hadn't have brought them into my life, and introduced me to them, I would have been none the wiser and she would have saved herself a small fortune. What can I say about my cousin, Suzi, except that I hope we never meet up in doggie Heaven, for that, excuse the pun, would be a fate worse than death. Yes, maybe I have been a little uppity at times, but one must remember, I had a royal name and, therefore, a royal status; so, what does one expect? Honestly, when I think back to that Hawaiian nonsense, I really don't know how Toni's mind worked half of the time; the other half of the time I don't think it was functioning at all, certainly not on all four cylinders. Toni…

As thoughts of Toni came crashing into my mind, I thought I heard a yelp in the far away distance, or was it my imagination or wishful thinking? I was already slipping off into the first stage of unconsciousness and starting to exit this mortal coil. But yes… I definitely heard it and there was no mistaking that hideous, high-pitched sound that pierced through my skull, and would do within a hundred-kilometre radius. It was… Suzi, of that there was no doubt. Slowly, I managed to turn my head; the only moveable part of my body, for all the other bits and pieces seemed to be in a state of paralysis. My heart leaped and pounded; never, ever, had I been so relieved to see Suzi and never, ever, was there so much love in my bursting heart for this gal. I stretched my eyes as far as possible and there she stood, at the edge of the lake, yelping, whining, barking and then, dash it all, wading into the cold, dark water and swimming towards me.

As I lay on my duvet that night, one eye on Toni, the tissue in her hand, mopping up either tears of joy or despair, I came to the conclusion that Suzi saved my life for a purpose and for one purpose only, she could not live without me; after all, who in their right mind could?

Summer brings with it the irresistible temptations of the hosepipe. I mean, how can a pooch possibly resist running after the snake-like structure, tugging at and pulling it until he caught it and firmly clung on to it with his choppers? It was certainly too much for me to resist, finally resulting in Toni banning me from having any further contact with this playful object. However, she doesn't know this; but, I am actually psyching myself up to try my luck again this summer.

I know you are dying to know how I got on with my venture, so how shall I proceed to tell you about the incident which eventually caused Toni, who was at the end of her tether, to impose a ten-metre boundary between the hosepipe and myself, much to my immense horror and complete annoyance?

It all started off brilliantly well. After a long winter and a cool spring, the weather was quickly picking up and graduating into long, sultry days. My mistress, as I have stated in previous chapters, was proud of her garden; so, watering was a must and a hosepipe, a necessity, to cover the area. The second I saw the long tube unwinding, I was fascinated and sat, like a statue, my eyes glued to the captivating, green serpent uncurling enticingly before my very eyes. Before I could stop myself, I sprang on to the magical coil trying desperately, without any luck, to capture the slithery tube between my teeth. As agile as I am, it was far too quick for me which actually made the whole process; or, should I say game, more exciting. Quickly, I pounced on the fast-escaping tube. It stopped for a brief moment; so did Toni.

"Kamehameha! What on Earth are you doing?" I heard her agitated cry from the end of the garden.

I was only interested in one thing and it certainly was not Toni's dilemma. The moment she resumed her unravelling, I resumed to partake in my most interesting challenge, my ears vaguely attune to a series of vague and incomprehensible gasps and sighs of desperation and my name being bandied about in none too sweet tones and certainly not pleasing to my ears. I ignored all her pleas and comments and persisted in my delightful quest. Every time my mistress pulled, tugged and tried, by any means possible, to straighten the curly pipe, I attacked it with all the ferocity I could muster, finally placing my paw on the slithering snake as an ultimate act of defiance. It was great fun to watch as it slowly began to slide away from me and I pounced again as it proceeded to slither away before my very eyes. This creature, I concluded, was alive and playful and very entertaining, but, best of all, it didn't answer back; and, so, the game continued. By now, I had my new found friend firmly in my teeth. There was a sharp tug. It was slithering away until I pounced on it again and gripped it with an added vigour. Oh, what fun! Briefly I turned my head, only to see Toni's head bobbing up and down as she shouted something or other in my direction and then, from the corner of my eye, I saw her unmistakable tree trunk legs. Don't, for goodness' sake tell her I said that, or I shall never hear the end of it; moreover, she'd put us both on some kind of weird diet. It will ever be my grim misfortune to experience. Well, back to the tree trunks, they were coming towards me, bigger and bigger they loomed; fast and furious their pace. I raised my head, the green slippery hose firmly attached to my pearly whites, only for my eyes to see a dark cloud covering Toni's face and I could see that she was not amused.

"Right young man; in you go." And, before I knew what was what, I was imprisoned in the house and could only dream about future hosepipe adventures.

Future adventures, however, did arise, with further bans imposed. Toni forgot her anger, only to find it again; but I never give in and to this day, my motto is: where there is a hosepipe, there is fun and I am ready, willing and waiting, as you will see when I finally get to the incident.

The hosepipe has all kinds of excellent qualities and one very attractive quality is its adaptability; for example, it can, with a certain amount of ingenuity, be miraculously transformed into an excellent water fountain, which is absolutely fantastic when one is thirsty on a hot, sultry day. Now, I know that I have always got water in the bowl and it's always fresh and cool; that's not the point and, anyway, where's the fun in just going up to the bowl and drinking the water? But, a hosepipe, well, that's another story. There is nothing more exciting than watching the cool, sparkling water gushing out a bit of tubing and catching it in my mouth. Toni hates this 'nonsense', as she calls it; for, not only do I get soaked to the skin, she does too; but I can't resist; I just can't resist. Sometimes I hear the water before I see it rising at the end of the long, flexible pipe and I sit, waiting patiently, though my body is tensed up in a state of high suspense, for the liquid to rush out and be caught in my eager mouth. Sometimes, however, it is only the odd drop; but, more often than not, its whole mouthfuls, which sometimes make me a bit sick and I end up spluttering, coughing and choking it all up.

"It serves you right, Kamehameha," I hear my frustrated mistress scold and maybe, for a few seconds, I agree with her admonishment until, that is, I recover and the whole process starts anew. I've lost count of the times I've been scolded, frowned upon, shouted at, imprisoned, and threatened with lifetime bans, knowing full well that all this negative, unnecessary behaviour on Toni's part is a waste of time and energy, for I am delighted to announce, there is always the next time.

My absolutely favourite game is the one which involves Toni manoeuvring the hosepipe between one plant and another and tries to outfox me. During this particular game, we often both get drenched and end up none too pleased with each other. On one such occasion, it kind of didn't go according to my plan and hence the incident.

I couldn't decide whether to go for the hosepipe or the water gushing out the end, both seemed very entertaining. Anyway, in my resolve not to miss out on any fun, I decided to go for both and, in my eagerness to do both justice, I accidentally gripped on the tube a little too hard and, to my amazement and delight, a second, much smaller, fountain was miraculously created, springing pleasingly from the flexible piping. This was magic indeed!

For a moment, I stood feeling both perplexed and fascinated. Mistakenly, I switched my eyes to Toni's red face, and was quick to notice there was no nice smile playing on her lips.

"Look what you have done, Kamehameha." She pointed her podgy forefinger to the mesmerising spring. I looked at it all right and I liked what I saw. Perhaps, I thought, I should create some more little fountains. A further glance at Toni's stony countenance told me this was not one of my best ideas and so I decided to place it on the back burner for the time being. Anyway, between the newly created spring, water gushing out of the end of the hose and the intricate weaving pattern my playful snake was designing, I was like a dog possessed running from one to the other and back again, entangling Toni in the pipe until… thud! She was in an untidy bundle on the ground. My curious eyes focussed firmly on her black, furious eyes and what I saw in these angry eyes didn't impress me at all; after all, we'd both had a lot of fun!

As I stared at my mistress's twisted torso, and the cool water flowing on and around her, I felt a strange twinge in my heart, for she did look a sorry sight. Perhaps, I had gone a little too far. My eyes jumped to the tempting spring flowing out the pipe and as I bent my head to take a delicious, refreshing mouthful, Toni decided to start disentangling herself, only to become further entangled and she and the pipe slithered ungainly towards the ground, her glaring eyes directly on me. I savoured the cool drops then, cautiously placing one foot in front of the other, I approached and perched beside the unsightly bundle, my ears attune to the sound of hearty laughter. I looked up and Toni, with her wet arms around me, buried her damp head in my soaking fur and howled with uncontrollable laughter as the water abundantly flowed out like a miniature Niagara Falls.

I thought that was the end of the matter; that Toni had seen the funny side and that all was forgiven and on the way to being forgotten; if only I had stopped there; if only I had somehow controlled my instinctive, fun-loving nature and walked away; but no, not me. As Toni rose, faffing around with the offending hose, I felt every vein in my body tingling with untold excitement, my heart raced in eager anticipation and I'm certain I could feel every little fur on my body standing on end and then… I went for it; catching the pipe, chewing, pulling, tugging and biting here, there and everywhere I could sink my teeth; my eyes as wide as plates as I saw fountain after fountain springing up the length of the hosepipe. What a delight! I pulled and tugged; barked, jumped, twirled and indulged in delicious sips; as did Toni, that is, apart from the barking and sipping. It all came to a sudden stop, when I looked around to see my mistress spread-eagled on the wet surface, and horrible threats coming my way. As for hoping she would forget, relent and forgive; forget it. Toni booked me in for a full shampoo and set and, to my complete horror, there was no get-out clause!

Autumn

Long summer days and short nights all too soon fall into autumn and, I feel, this season brings with it joy and pleasure, as well as an underlying sense of sadness and, this year, a very unpleasant occurrence.

Once Toni had acquired her new kitchen, which I told you about in a previous chapter, it opened up a whole new world for me; for now I could enjoy the delights autumn had on offer from the warmth and comfort of the indoors. At this time of the year, there is nothing better than to sit sedately in the comfort of one's castle and marvel at the autumnal delights which never fail to bring me a source of untold pleasure. The colourful yellow, red, russet, purple and orange leaves always put on a spectacular show; some of the dying foliage, I have noticed, is tinged with black and lingering bits of green as it twirls and whirls in the cool air; sometimes they collide; mostly, however, their dying dance is solitary as they, one by one, flutter and float in a descending spiral. How they enchant me; oh, how I wish I could join them.

Join them I did on occasion; sometimes on my own; sometimes with Toni walking by my side. And, what displays we witnessed, for, the rich, jewel-like colours were everywhere: beneath us as we crunched and crackled our way through the colourful carpet; above us desperately clinging on to the skeletal branches as if their very lives depended on them; landing on us before they performed their final dances of farewell and gracefully spiralled down to their resting place. I particularly loved them floating on to my golden-white coat, for they made me feel a part of their exquisite and mesmerising dance and as they said their last silent farewell I felt a deep, overwhelming sadness creeping over me; but, somehow, deep inside, I knew it had to be this way.

Now, I come to something unpleasant, which I certainly was not expecting and neither, I knew, was Toni. As I recall, we were walking back home after we had both enjoyed a brisk walk. It was dark, cold and the wind was howling in the trees. Suddenly, I froze, my four feet stuck to the ground and unable to move this way or that, as my eyes grew wide at the spectacle before me. Was it human; a monster of some kind; or indeed, some kind of fiend from the darkest, deepest depths of Hell? Was it the devil himself? My stark eyes stuck firmly on the ghastly vision before me, as I tried to make some kind of sense of what I was seeing. I must hasten to add; when I last perceived Toni, before I became fixated on the creature; she seemed completely oblivious to it all. Is she blind, or in a world of her own, as she so often is? I wondered. I felt the tug of my lead, obviously a hint to move forward; but, no cigar, I was firmly stuck with my eyes firmly on the monstrosity. Desperately, I was trying to formulate what kind of beast I was gawping at, for I am glad to say that my intelligent brain was still, thankfully, functioning; though, maybe not at full capacity. I noticed that this thing had a human body; though, his horrific face was a sickly green, with tinges of darkest black, interspersed with shades of red and grey; the eyes were large, black pools and around their edges were jagged yellow lines and zigzags; the cavernous mouth was misshapen and grotesque in its twisted form and it was blood red with, what looked like, drops of blood spurting out the crevices. I felt another tug; but, this pooch was not for moving. And then I felt a tenseness in Toni's body as out of nowhere, it seemed, another hideous creature sprang out before us, visibly displaying the human skeletal form and the skull showing gnashers which grinned inanely. This monster pranced around, waving his bony arms erratically in Toni's face while, at the same time, making hideous noises, forcing Toni to shrink backwards and lean her trembling body against a rough, prickly hedge. I managed, somehow, to raise my eyes to her and could see the fear in her eyes. Leaning against her, I could feel her body tremble, as the skeleton thrust his hand in her bewildered face.

"Trick or treat… trick or treat?" His ghastly looking choppers grinned as the masked creature joined in and both continued their repetitive litany, like an old scratched vinyl. "Trick or treat… trick or treat…"

"G-go away; I h-haven't got any m-money," I heard my petrified mistress stammer.

"Then it will be a trick, lady." The skeleton laughed raucously.

Toni attempted to edge her way around the two idiots as my eyes strayed to them. Clearly, they weren't going to give up. I continued to sense Toni's body tensing more and more; I could almost hear her heart thumping as I was beginning to understand that this scene was not normal and was not to be tolerated. Before I did something I would regret, I decided to wait and see what was going to happen; hoping that we could depart the location without any retaliation; but, as I stared into their ugly countenances, I knew it wasn't to be, as they continued to jeer, laugh, snarl and, to my horror, poke fingers and sticks at Toni.

I could stand no more; my own fear quickly dissipating as I tugged sharply, escaped from Toni's grasp and went directly for their heels. I pinched and nipped as they hopped from one foot to the other, like two cats on burning coals; the cold, dark air full of their curses, threats and words I'd rather not repeat if I was to stay in Toni's good books.

Suffice it to say, all I could see was the luminous skeleton running for his life, before they both vanished into the dark of the night. As for a reward, all I wanted was to feel safe and sound in the company of my brave owner.

I learned, soon after that incident, that it was the time of year for wearing strange costumes and masks; Halloween; or, something like that, it's called. I've also heard it said that most of the time it's innocent, harmless fun. I must admit at taking a liking to the long, pointed hats the so-called witches wear; but if I see one of their black cats…

Bonfire Night, as I have mentioned in an earlier chapter, is not so much fun for me. To this very day, and well into my grand old age in doggie years, I am petrified of the loud bangs, whizzing, whistles and minor explosions and have to take the dreaded p—i—l—l— s to calm down. Such is life!

Winter

I am not too sure, at this stage of my life on this planet, if winter is a delight or a curse. As with all the seasons, it's got its good points and its bad points; on the whole, if it wasn't for all the fuss that comes with this season, I think I would favour it.

I must say, being stuck indoors for days at a time is no joy, especially when Toni decides to escalate our heating system to full blast. Can you imagine sitting in a thick, fur coat, under a scorching sun; well, that's how I feel. Let me tell you, it's no fun. Needless to say, I get irritable, I yap rather a lot and I snooze more than I should and dream of summer days when the hosepipe is in full flow. I hate the short days, the bare gardens, stark fields and human beings continually complaining to each other about the abysmal weather. Toni; however, does not engage in the art of complaining. She is now in the throes of planning some sort of grand event, which is to take place towards the end of December. What it is, I do not know; but, together with Auntie Anusia, they sit and talk for hours about it, go out on excursions, returning with mysterious bags full of odd looking glittery, colourful balls I wouldn't mind getting my paws on and shiny, long, stringy type of things; goodness only knows what they are going to do with all of this stuff.

Then there are strange aromas coming from our kitchen. I've seen a large, brown, spotty type of cake being wrapped, then, after some days, unwrapped to have something exchanged for a pungent smelling liquid injected into it, then wrapped again and placed in a large tin, only for the process to be repeated again and again. I mean, what is the point of all that rigmarole? Surely, if a delicious cake is made, the only sensible thing for a human, not to mention a pooch, is to devour and enjoy.

If these were the only weird things happening it wouldn't be too bad; but then I was thrown into further confusion and… trouble.

Toni and Auntie Anusia spent one whole day going up and down the stairs, like two demented yo-yos, descending with large boxes, packages and bags, which were all bursting at the seams and planted them down erratically wherever they found a space with no thought, it seemed, for my comfort; or, indeed, safety. There I was, in the midst of all this paraphernalia, with no escape route and only a sufficient amount of room to perch down; I could forget about sprawling out, it wasn't an option. There were boxes of all sizes in front, behind and on either side of me; it was a pure miracle one wasn't sitting on my head. And there I was, King Kamehameha, in the midst of all this chaos and madness, trying to look serene, untouched and, above all, regal. To these boxes, bigger and bulkier boxes were added. I didn't even attempt to get cosy and comfortable; for, as a fool would see, it was a futile venture; however, after a lot of scrambling about, my paws causing something to crackle, amazingly, I managed to recline, be it in a crumbled heap. I closed my eyes tightly and begged for sleep to take over. "Ho… ho… ho…" My eyes stark, like saucers, flitted erratically around the chaos surrounding me: above, beneath, to one side and then another; but, I could see no one. The 'ho… ho… hos' were getting louder and were starting to antagonise my fragile nerves. "Ho… ho… ho…" My confused eyes switched from one box, to bag, to bulging package to seek out the dastardly culprit. "Ho… ho… ho…" Enough was enough! Up I sprang, like a Jack-in-the-box, my paws ascending up and descending down everything in my way, my long and inquisitive nose in every nook and cranny. "Ho… ho… ho…" Crack! Pop! Snap! Relentlessly, I marched, determined in my quest to hunt down the transgressor, for I was on a mission and in the footsteps of my namesake, the Great King Kamehameha. I was not about to give up. Over boxes and packages, I continued to climb, my ears finely attune to the cracking, snapping and popping noises; in fact, I was starting to enjoy myself when the sound of tinkling glass, as it intermingled with the other delightful sounds, added to the ambience of it all. And soon, bags, boxes… creaking… packages… crackling… tubes… popping and not forgetting myself, were one happy and glorious mess. What fun!

"Kamehameha!"

I froze. Abruptly my fun ended; Toni's furious glance confirmed the matter.

"Kamehameha!"

Actually, I heard her the first time; I just wasn't ready to face the dire consequences. Time stood still, as did I, for what seemed like eons with only one sign of life coming from some mysterious hidden box. "Ho… ho… ho…" I awaited my dismal fate, for I recognised that black look on my mistress's face and this time, she had the cavalry behind her; for Auntie Anusia did not look too pleased either. I was, I knew, in deep water with no life boat to rescue me from my gloomy predicament. I was well and truly stuck in the middle of all the mayhem and the evidence of my crime was all around me as it stared us all in the face. I heard Toni's sigh of both utter frustration and resignation.

Auntie Anusia sort of came to my rescue, though I felt she could have tried a little harder on my behalf. "Not to worry, he may not have broken anything of value."

Toni waved her hands in total despair and cast her dagger-like eyes directly at me. "But, everything is of value; it's all sentimental stuff; it all means… meant everything to me."

I stood, unmovable, in the midst of the chaos and, as I surreptitiously glanced at Toni's watery eyes, my heart went out to her. I knew I'd done something wrong; but what, I couldn't for the life of me fathom out. "Ho… ho… ho…" came the infuriating sound. "Ho… ho… ho…"

"Oh, for crying out loud, let me get at the scoundrel!"

Another look at her firmly set mouth, her eyes of freezing ice glaring at me told me, in no uncertain terms, that my mistress was about to commit murder in the first degree. "Ho… ho… ho…" Her eyes flitted from me to the source of the trouble, a tiny hope of clemency hanging in the air, as I stared at the culprit; a small figure dressed in red with a long, flowing beard on his chubby, red cheeked face; the real perpetrator, who was the cause of these fragmented baubles, snapped shiny bits of tinsel and misshapen paper chains of sentimental value. Toni's eyes switched to me, as I trembled beneath my cool exterior and, together with Auntie Anusia, they broke out into a hearty bout of hysterical laughter as I stood motionless, entangled from head to paws in strands of red, gold and silver strands of tinsel, a blob of red glitter on my nose.

"Rudolph!" Toni managed to exclaim pointing her podgy finger at me, as she plonked herself down amongst the festive debris, retrieving a headless angel, before being overtaken by another bout of irrepressible laughter.

And, whoever Rudolph and his employer are, I think they saved my skin!

I saw strange things ascending, for example, a snow-covered tree, adorned with lots of shiny baubles and that shiny tinsel stuff. I must admit, it looked beautiful, as did the entire house, decked with lush garlands; Holly and Ivy decked the fire place and the window sills; red plants in pots were scattered decorously around the place and the spicy aroma emitted from festive candles was very intoxicating. It was all very charming indeed; but, what it was all here for, I didn't quite understand.

During this time, there were special tasting sessions and those I loved the most. I loved to sample, and savour, the rich brandy laced mince pies, with crumbling pastry which just broke and melted in my mouth and turkey, my absolute favourite; delicious! Now and again, a sample of freshly made marzipan or rich fruit cake would pass my way; the rest of the time, I passed the time of day by dreaming of more festive treats to come my way.

A few days before the Great Day itself, mysterious covered boxes and packages were decorously wrapped in shiny paper, with matching bows, and placed around the elegant tree. Now I knew, from my recent experience, that touching boxes and packages meant trouble; but, being the inquisitive pooch I am, I couldn't help casting secret glances their way; but, no way was I going to touch them; however, each time I passed these alluring parcels, the temptation was rising to an unbearable degree. There was no sound emitting from any of them; but, there was a strong aroma, of something quite familiar, from one of them and another pleasing smell, I couldn't quite put my paw on, from another source. Whatever these smells were, and wherever they were coming from, were covered and firmly sealed; but still, there was no denying the fact that something very tasty lay beneath. I passed these annoyingly enticing temptations several times a day, for, I hasten to add, the ban on wandering through the house was temporarily lifted during this important season, and as a result my curiosity grew stronger each time. I knew I was playing with fire; but, whatever it was in those hidden packages, smelt absolutely delicious and I wanted it desperately. On Christmas Eve, it all became too much for me, and instead of walking past, like my strong-willed namesake would have surely done, I diverted and headed straight for the delectable aroma. I nudged my curious nose in; further and further it went. There was no denying it, there were some very tasty treats somewhere and they smelt like my favourites! Crashing into my mind came flashbacks of my recent escapade, amidst the boxes and packages and hastily I retrieved my nose, and person, from the source of the tempting aromas. It wasn't easy; I tried very hard to avoid, walk away and forget and I did all three, only to return and stick my nose where it shouldn't have been. As I was playing detective, a brilliant idea raced into my intelligent head. If the packages were intended for me, and clearly they were; for, I couldn't imagine Toni digging her choppers into my marrowbones, then I would be justified in tearing the parcels and devouring their contents; and, that's exactly what I did.

I don't quite remember the sequence of events which followed. I opened my eyes to a long, white overcoat and a stern looking v—e—t peering down on me as I lay motionless on Toni's sofa feeling woozy, drunk and not myself at all; in fact, at that moment in time, I wouldn't have minded leaving this mortal coil. It was not to be. I was to live and, not only that, but I had some glorious form of punishment waiting in store for me; for, not only had I spoilt Toni's Christmas Day, the emergency v—e—t was giving my mistress a white envelope, the contents within I knew only too well I was not going to enjoy; not to mention the hefty bill which would wing its way through the door in the near future and, no doubt, affect my treats in some way or another. To top it all off, I don't even know if it was all worth it; for, apart from the v—e—t and my hangover, I can't remember a thing!

I would like to meet the person who invented cameras and, when I do, it would not be to thank him. Cameras are a curse I cannot abide. I know I am beautiful; some would even go so far as to say that I'm elegant and charming and, therefore, photogenic, and I certainly wouldn't disagree with them; but, the sight of that ghastly invention sends me crazy. I cannot explain why cameras send me into lunatic mode; but, there it is; I hate them!

Recently, I have been watching Toni pointing the atrocious contraption here, there and everywhere as she tried to capture the festive season in all its glory; that's all right, so long as she doesn't point the thing at me. By now I had recovered from my recent tryst with the v—e—t and, to make amends with my beloved Toni, I was desperately trying to be super good. I knew, from past experiences, my mistress liked me sitting pretty and so I obliged, and, to my delight, won a couple of treats and then… SNAP, and before I knew what was happening, she had captured me in time; so, to this very day, our eventful Christmas has been immortalised in an over-elaborate silver frame, which I have to pass on my way to bed.

The white stuff; snow, I think, they call it; now, there's a thing to get your paws stuck into; it's cool, soft, sometimes crunchy, at other times brown-grey and slushy; but, whatever its colour or state, it never fails to be a source of fun. Its sole drawback is its attractive appeal as it, inevitably, brings out the dreaded camera and all that it entails. But, never again; one festive shot is one too many and I firmly protest using my skills of yapping, running around in monotonous circles, nipping Toni's heels until I'm sent straight to my bed in a state of disgrace, any treats hiding in my blanket, hastily withdrawn.

So, as I reflect on the four seasons, if I was pressed to choose a favourite, I would have to choose summer; for, with it comes freedom of spirit and the spirit of life is living it to the full.

Chapter Fourteen
Things Sent to Make My Life a Misery

There are many things in this world, and probably the next, which, I feel, are sent to make my life a misery; a few of these things send me straight into orbit and Toni into a state of frustrated, undiluted rage.

Bins, according to my intelligent mind, should have a worldwide ban enforced upon them. I am not drawn to their appearance because, as we all know, they are often dirty, smelly and certainly not aesthetically pleasing to the eye. The slightest sound of their movements sends me into a spiral of negative behaviour, some would say bordering on lunacy. I don't know what it is about them; for, they don't screech, scratch or grind in any way; but, if anyone happens to move them a mere centimetre I'm on to them; usually Toni and the bin, and before you know it, there's a full-blown fight between the offending bin, Toni and myself; all striving desperately to win the battle.

On one such occasion, a green bin was full to the brim with trash; I was at the bottom of the garden, calmly surveying my kingdom when Toni, surreptitiously, attempted to move the bin. Not a good idea when I'm on the horizon and she should have known better; but then, she is not as intelligent as I; for, in a flash, I was pounding up the stepping stones at top speed and in seconds, hands, feet, fur, paws, bodies and the bin were flying erratically around, with my growling techniques added to the mix.

"Get off, Kamehameha… Kamehameha… off!"

To no avail; my ears, mind and will were firmly opposed to her urgent pleas, for, I had a plan of my very own and, anyway, this was starting to be great fun as I barked, grabbed, pulled, tugged and growled at the bin, which was by now balancing precariously on one unsteady wheel, then another. For a split moment, it balanced perfectly and Toni thought she'd got the upper hand; but, in my brilliant mind, never presume or assume, or take anything for granted in this life. My theory has been proved right on many occasions and never more so than in this particular incident. For a few seconds, I ceased my incessant growling and raised my eyes to the bin. I moved. Toni moved. The bin moved and my mistress started wobbling all over the place. Desperately she tried to, somehow, balance on one foot, her grasping hand trying to grab the handle of the bin, while the unyielding object swayed this way and that; on one wheel and then another. This was my chance. I contemplated no more and made a bid to conquer the bin, resuming my growling and barking as my whole body moved in one direction, then another.

"A… ah!" I heard my mistress, as I nipped her on her heel as she had impolitely trodden on my paw. The bin hobbled and toppled, the lid by now wide open, and the contents escaping as I trampled on the knotted plastic carriers full of rubbish, on Toni's toes, on an empty chicken curry carton, which had all absconded from their carriers, as I continued to growl and bark at the top of my voice and then it happened…

As if in slow motion, Toni, I, the dishonourable bin, and its trash, all ended up sprawled out on the ground. Momentarily, I switched my eyes to my mistress and there she was, spread out on the surface, with bits of old potato peeling, egg shells, yogurt cartons and stale, mouldy bread, covering my Toni as she lay motionless amongst the scattered, smelly litter; the bin, by now, also motionless, lying on its side like a beached whale. Involuntarily, my eyes squinted as her eyes of black thunder darted to me; her mouth set in a firm line, silent and mutinous and not at all friendly. What can a level headed pooch do in such dire circumstances? My brain whizzed and whirled; and then it came to me! Slowly, I padded over old crisp packets, chocolate and sweet wrappers; so much for her healthy regime, I thought, in passing as I slowly placed one cautious foot in front of the other and approached my furious mistress, planted myself next to her and sat amongst the scattered debris as I awaited my fate with bated breath.

I felt the warmth of her arm around me; saw her fling an old banana skin into the air; heard her hysterical laughter and instinctively, I knew, we were still the best of friends; as for the offending bin, it too was forgiven.

Salad spinners; another inflicted vice on society and something to ruffle any pooch's peaceful state of mind. Thankfully, at first, I only had to suffer this particular torture on a rare occasion, when my mistress decided to go on one of her diet fads involving salads and the need for a spinner. The problem is, Toni is not like a normal person spinning the salad stuff for a few rounds; for some ludicrous reason, known only to her, she has to spin one hundred and nineteen times. Now do you believe me when I tell you she's nuts? Anyway, this salad spinner, it's like Chinese torture; immediately as the grinding starts, my ears prick up, momentarily every single muscle in my body tenses up and, before I'm aware of what I'm doing, I'm pounding from wherever I am to the source of the sound at top speed. Into the kitchen I go barking, jumping around, barking more; running around in circles, jumping more and, in the process, sending Toni off into some kind of orbit of her own as she snaps and shouts at me. Stop spinning, woman, I'm barking, as she continues her excruciating torture. Eventually, after her one hundredth and nineteenth spin, she mercifully stops and all is peaceful again, until the next time. Maybe I wouldn't mind all the fuss so much if what she was spinning was worth the agony; but, lettuce, tomatoes, radishes, onions and other vegetables are nothing to rave over, as far as I am concerned.

Now, I know tasty treats are put near the door to entice me inside and if it's a choice between treats and freedom, the latter always wins. To my utter dismay, Toni cottoned on to this salad spinner and its magic powers, for she realised that when I flatly refuse to go inside the house and nothing lures me in, then it's time for a few rounds of the ghastly contraption and, begrudgingly, I am well and truly inside.

Toni does not use an appropriate jar opener to open stubborn lids. Oh no; instead, when she can't get at her jam, honey or pickled onions, out comes a knife with a sturdy metal handle and there she is, heartily banging on the lid; this, I need to point out, does not do my blood pressure any good, especially when she usually commences this procedure when I'm in the middle of a most delightful dream; a fight ensues and once again, we're in the fur and temper ruffled zone.

Another annoyance of mine is being forced to walk on a particular side, when Toni and I are partaking in a leisurely stroll. I feel most comfortable, and at ease, when I am walking with my right side to Toni's left side. Toni has been okay with this and she has accommodated this little whim of mine until just recently; she has noticed that where my lead has been constantly rubbing against my right side, it has caused my fur to snap and I am left with a small, but visible, rather flat patch of fur. Myself, I would forego aesthetics at this point, opting for comfort; but, no, Toni is now insisting I walk on her right side and I don't like this arrangement one little bit; so, as a consequence, we are constantly switching positions, trying to have our own way, leaving us both totally frazzled, especially when I suddenly swerve to her left side, trying to get back to my rightful position, and she's trying tactfully to manoeuvre me back. It's an on-going battle, I fear, neither of us shall win.

"No, Kamehameha," I hear her protest.

Yes, I am thinking, as I forcibly attempt to get back on my favourite side.

On one such occasion, as I manoeuvred back to her left, she tripped over me and we both spiralled downwards and ended up in a graceless heap.

Frost and polished floors belong in this category. I hate them both. I have noticed on many occasions, when Toni and I go off on our winter walks, she shares my problem of balancing on frosty, icy pavements. When I'm tired of slipping and sliding all over the place, I simply give up, sit down for a while and enjoy a nice little respite; I'm kind of waiting for Toni to cotton on to this brilliant idea and do the same thing.

I sigh deeply, unrivalled fear surging through my veins, when I see a polished wooden floor; for some inexplicable reason, I just can't seem to get a grip on them. I try by cautiously placing one foot in front of the other and venturing on to the shiny surface, only to find that I am well and truly stuck; or, slipping and sliding in every direction, unable to put a foot forward or back and as for going sideways, forget it. So, I stand there, like an immortalised statue, waiting for I don't know what; eventually, I either summon up courage to venture further; or, somehow, reverse backwards into the boundary surface on to a relative safe and secure patch.

Passing traffic is a curse and motorists, I have noticed, have no regard of preserving one's tranquillity, when one is in the process of enjoying a casual stroll; perhaps enjoying a daydream too, when… whizz… out of the blue, something loud, fast and furious, like an angry beast, goes roaring by. My blood boils and there is no stopping me at this point as I whirl and twirl about; yapping, barking and generally causing a minor disturbance, while poor Toni is desperately clinging on to the end of the lead, as if her very life depended on it. She twirls and whirls with me, with a curse of her own thrown in for good measure; although, I must admit, I'm not sure if the curse is intended for the motorist or myself; anyway, whoever it's intended for, the whole scenario is definitely not a pretty sight.

I know I have mentioned this in the previous chapter; but, I am still camera shy. Yes, I am well aware it goes totally against the grain. I am photogenic; a model dog with my beautiful, almond-shaped, dark brown eyes to die for; my stance firm and straight, my gorgeous sable and white coat and my usual expression of wisdom, high intelligence and perfection all make me a most suitable candidate for one of the top doggie magazines; but, the mere sight of a camera and… whoosh… I'm gone! Subconsciously, I think, I may possess the ancient North American Indian fear of believing my spirit may be stolen when my image is taken and, who in their right mind, wants to tempt fate? Saying this, Toni has many images of me, taken under duress, scattered around the house in silver frames and my youthful spirit is still very much intact.

So, yes, there are many curses and obstacles in this life that one must try and avoid at all costs. If they are unavoidable, and suffer them you must, then at all costs make sure you, somehow, turn them to your advantage and then life with humans may be bearable; if not enjoyable.

Chapter Fifteen
Potential Suitors

You may well ask at whom this particular chapter is directed. You would get two very different answers; for, I would automatically insist that Toni needs a man; but not just any old thing; Toni, on the other hand, would argue that I need a wife and I don't think she's too fussed about who would take me away; in fact, on occasion, when she's caught me on one of my off days, she's even threatened to pack my meagre belongings and send me off to Suzi, I must say, I can think of a host of much better wives I'd rather spend the rest of my days with. Actually, I did very briefly think of Suzi in a wifely role, after she had saved me from my watery grave, but, you know what happened there. I must confess, there have been other potential candidates I have had my eyes on, but these have turned out to be either too high maintenance for my liking, like the self-possessed Poodle I mentioned in the Heavenly Home Kennels; or, other unsuccessful candidates that have not been spruced up enough for my exceptionally high standards. A potential wife, in my esteemed consideration, would be one who would walk a pace or two behind me; certainly not in front; for, I will not allow any pooch, no matter how gorgeous, to steal my limelight.

A pooch who willingly shares her treats and toys may have a chance; though, one necessary qualification is a pooch who allows me to be the chief taster with any form of sausages, pieces of roast chicken, pork, beef or any other delicious meaty morsels.

I need a good-looking gal who would complement my handsome looks, but not overshadow them in any way with her own eye-catching appearance; a lady pooch who would look up to me for guidance and leadership and fall in with my plans, whatever they may be. Above all, my wife would never, ever, dream of getting close to my Toni; she is exclusive only to me.

So far, finding such a rare jewel has been a fruitless quest; so, I continue to live my solitary, bachelor life with my eyes firmly peeled on the talent around.

Toni, however, is a whole different issue. She would never admit it; but, I think, she is secretly scanning the outer periphery for a possible suitor. She, of course, as I have heard with my own ears, denies and laughs off such notions as she states to her friends, "… A ludicrous idea…" with other statements like, "I haven't got any time for a man… too busy… don't want to wash any guy's socks and, God forbid, his underpants!" She has no need to talk; to this very day, she has the audacity to hang a stream of ghastly, oversized pants on the washing line for all to see. I tell you, a man with a grain of sense in his head would run, and never look back, after witnessing such monstrosities. Anyway, it's all rubbish! The lady protests far too much and too loud. She wants a man; but, no one will have such a fusspot; not if they want to stay sane!

And so we plod on, two singletons in search of true love. Actually, I have secretly looked for potential suitors for my mistress. I have observed, inspected and assessed them one by one and, so far, none of them have attained my meticulous standards. I mean, you mustn't forget my role in all of this. Above all, I cannot contemplate the slightest possibility of being usurped, for that truly would be a fate worse than death itself. So, any chap who dares to venture into the lion's den is a brave chap indeed; for, he has to get past me. Now, if you are wondering what this last statement is all about, let me explain this with a little more detail. If a treat is not visible on a potential suitor's approach, he can forget getting past me; or, even think about getting me on side. The best thing for such an imprudent candidate to do is turn and retreat at top speed. Secondly, if he does happen to be a wise character, worth his salt so to speak, he needs to compliment me on my good looks and, if he pats and strokes me, so much the better and, who knows, if I'm in a good mood I might even offer him my paw as a sign of initial friendship. Notice, the operative word here is 'initial', for he has other tests to pass before he can start to think he has a chance. However, once he has managed to graduate past the gate and ventured through the door, he needn't get it into his head that he's home and dry. Oh no… no… no… If he thinks he can just make himself comfortable and ignore me as part of the fixtures and furniture, then he can jolly well think again. Don't forget, he will need my continual approval if he is allowed to stay, that means I shall be closely observing, monitoring and assessing his every move.

An important issue is one of positioning oneself appropriately on the sofa or chair. This is an extremely important manoeuvre and not one to be taken lightly, for many have failed in this area and not taken precious time to think of their strategies with minute precision. Firstly, let's start with the chair. When Toni and her man are sat at the kitchen table, he needn't think I should be banned from the area, nudged into a corner somewhere out of sight and sound or ignored in any way at all. I need to be firmly in the middle, in the centre of proceedings, next to Toni, where I can adequately continue to observe and assess the important potentiality of my prospective dad.

Food is an extremely important matter. When we are at the table, I need to be given a tasty morsel now and then; well really at regular intervals, if all is to run smoothly. If our guest fails in this most vital of obligations, then it's curtains for him; selfish, greedy suitors who are only concerned with their own stomach and have no thought for their host are not in the rating. Suitors need to be most obliging and generous to a fault; otherwise, it's goodbye and good riddance!

Suitors of a particular eager romantic persuasion are advised to tread carefully; again many have tried and failed miserably, or so Toni has led me to believe; personally, I have not seen them queuing at the door. Again, if a guy is so intrepid as to venture this far, he will immediately notice that I am always at Toni's side. Oh, I nearly forgot to mention, on these very rare occasions, she allows me into my castle. Don't ask me what causes this delightful turn of events, all I know is I make the most of these, once in a blue moon, situations. Anyway, back to the romance bit. When they get to the canoodling part, I am there by my mistress's side. It is an absolute must that her intended makes room for me to nudge in so that I can be part of the proceedings, woe-betide if he leaves me out of the loop; for, it will be sudden death to any further romantic notions he may have.

Now, apart from giving her my consent, Toni does have some say in the matter; but, I must say, potential suitors come and go and neither I, nor Toni, have been suitably impressed; still, we keep looking and… hoping!

Chapter Sixteen
The Time When...

The time when… Please don't ask me to elaborate on this topic until the time I have fully recovered (which may never come to pass!)

Chapter Seventeen
Ageing: A Most Delightful Process

Ageing is a dreadful word for many. Not for my mistress, Toni; as far as she's concerned, she refuses to get old. To be honest with you, I'm not quite sure if she's ever grown up; whether she has, indeed, entered into her second childhood; or, maybe, she truly has the Hawaiian spirit she claims to possess. Whatever the case may be, I must agree that she is certainly young in spirit.

In body, I'm not so sure. She tries, poor soul; but, hair extensions, at sixty-four… really? And, as for nail extensions, don't get me started on that topic. Suffice it to say, they should be banned. They get stuck in my fur and because of this, she tugs at my coat to get the despicable things out; not to mention the whole day I was walking around with one of these despicable things entangled in my fur coat and she was frantically searching the house, from top to bottom, trying to find it because, she says, she can't be seen with a nail missing. I'm sure I've even swallowed one offending article after she had lost it in my food.

Fitness; now there's another topic. She could do with getting fit and she tries; but, honestly, I don't see any difference. She's still the same 'old' Toni; a bit too cuddly in all the wrong places. She's too stingy to spend money on the gym; or, go swimming, like any other normal person would do; so, I have to watch her attempting, in vain, to keep up with the exercise tutor on the television screen and listen to her gasps, sighs, puffing and panting and never to be repeated exclamations; not to mention the much shorter walks I usually get after one of her sessions.

Diets; well I think I've already mentioned them in passing and, as far as I am concerned, the least said on this ghastly subject the better. All I am going to say here is that when she's not on a diet, I have some hope of tucking into my square meals, plus doggie treats.

Now, I've worked out that in doggie years my Toni would be off the scale and that's all I'm going to say, if I want to live. I, on the other hand, am in my late fifties; a grand age, if only I was allowed to grow old gracefully. Take, for example, our walks. I would rather partake in a long, leisurely stroll befitting the status of a king. Oh no… no… no… She drags me off on brisk walks because, apparently, she's heard or read somewhere that brisk walks have some sort of health benefits. Well, these health benefits are not evident to me; she arrives on the doorstep, puffing and panting and I am ready to snooze for England!

Talking of snoozing; it's my favourite pastime and I'm ready for a good, old snooze any time and any place. Toni is having none of this and when I do try and catch forty winks, she jabbers on, calls my name and moves me on. Now, I ask you, how is a guy supposed to catch up on his beauty sleep with this rumpus going on in the background? After all, if she had more sleep herself, she'd probably get that beauty thing right because, let's face it, nothing else seems to work. Another thing; when I'm in a state of relaxation, pondering on the mysteries of life, she asks me inane questions and, what's more, I think she expects me to answer her. "Kamehameha, what are you up to… what do you think… let's see, Kamehameha, should we…?" If I could answer her back, believe me, I would and tell her, in no uncertain terms, to give me some peace.

Each evening, there are night time rituals I have to endure. After our evening walk, she bestows on me a chicken strip and disappears; where, I do not know. Anyway, I settle down to sleep, only to be interrupted an hour or two later when she reappears, makes her tea, grabs a chocolate bar (I'm saying nothing!) and disappears again. Granted, she always gives me another doggie treat; but, why on Earth can't she do all her jobs in one go so I can have some undisturbed shut-eye? It would, if she'd only think about it, save her a lot of unnecessary hassle too; but, then she hasn't got my brain so I'll forgive her for this nonsense.

Health; I don't particularly want to dwell on this topic because, with it, comes the dreaded visions of the v—e—t and his mysterious white packages. I must confess, my joints hurt a little; I'm not as agile as I used to be; my teeth are not the brilliant white they once were and I'm saying no more. As for Toni, I hope she never has any ailments and lives forever.

Now, to be quite honest with you, so far, I am finding the ageing process quite delightful. I think of myself as a handsome, super intelligent, mature and wise 'old' pooch; a model amongst models. I expect to be treated with the utmost of respect and care and, of course, to be spoiled whenever the opportunity arises.

Needless to say, I love being admired, complimented and worshipped by family, friends and admirers so I would like to say to all of my subjects, just keep doing what you are doing and I'll be happy.

And, so I gracefully slip into my next phase of life with no apprehension; rather, I look forward to a host of further pleasures and adventures life has to offer. Naturally, I shall slow down a bit; but, in a graceful, sedate way; a way that all will admire.

I aim to do as little as I can get away with; though, guarding my kingdom, I feel, is not a duty; rather it is a great privilege.

I have got no notion of abandoning Toni in her dotage; for, as I have hinted before, I don't think she could live without me; her life would certainly not be the same!

So, old age, bring it on. King Kamehameha is ready and waiting.

Chapter Eighteen
The Time When...

After months of mulling over the unfortunate incident, I think I am just about ready to share my horrific experience; only, may I hasten to add, because it ended quite satisfactorily for me and on reflection, though not a word of this to Toni, the torture of it all was well worth the rewards I later consequently received and enjoy to this present day.

The wind is totally to blame, for, had it not been for the force of nature, none of what I am about to relate would have happened and neither I, nor my mistress, would have aged ten years in the space of a week.

The day began in its usual way with an early morning brisk walk, breakfast and all the usual nonsensical fuss Toni makes as she prepares herself to meet the world. You know the kind of things I mean: the application of make-up, straightening hair, making sure everything worn is colour coordinated and so on. Anyway, finally, Toni was on her way to work and I was looking forward to a luxurious, undisturbed snooze and the prospect of tucking into yummy treats, for being a good pooch, on her return and so I settled down on my ancient blanket, closed my eyes and willed blissful sleep to take me for its own. It did and what a dream I had! There were rabbits intermingling with cats where, one minute, I was chasing a family of rabbits and the next minute I was licking my lips at the prospect of having cat for my next meal, with a generous portion of a rich, meaty sauce on top, when suddenly…

I raised one eye. Everything in the kitchen was as it should be. Pots washed and cleared away, the worktops sparkling clean; everything in its place and a place for everything, as they say, and yet something strange was occurring. My ears pricked up at the whooshing, whirling, hissing sound. In an instant, I was on my feet and at the window, where my unblinking eyes stared at the commotion; my whole body started to tremble at… at what, I don't know… the terrible swishing sound outside, the branches of the trees tossing frantically this way and that; mingling, intermingling, weaving in and out of each other as they danced their frenzied dance and all the while I stood frozen, entranced and transfixed; for there, in the corner of my eye, hanging on precariously to a sturdy wavy branch was a… cat. Convinced he was one of the cats in my dream, almost fated to be my supper; I was bewitched by the silly fellow; for you cannot, in your right mind, assume he is clever to venture on such a mission in a gale force wind. Anyway, at this point of the proceedings, I didn't know what I wanted the stupid creature to do; for if he, somehow, managed to plant himself back on terra firma, he would surely disappear and the prospect of cat inside my tummy would disappear with him; if he broke his neck, he would quickly be disposed of, one way or another, on Toni's return, and if he stayed, I would be left with the arduous task of hunting the blighter down and that to me, felt too much like hard work. Anyway, while I was pondering on these matters, my eyes were firmly peeled on this lithe imbecile who, by the wind, was tossed this way and that, like an oversized, irregular shaped, unfortunate leaf. Actually, I must say, I was quite amused watching his antics, as he clung on to the branch for dear life, his eyes turning this way and that, trying to find a means of escape. Suddenly, his eyes caught mine and miraculously, to my dismay, he instantly plucked up enough courage to scamper down the unruly branch on to another less sturdy branch, where the weight of him propelled the branch to snap and it, and its cargo, fall ungainly to the ground whereupon, at that moment, my own excitement grew to fever point. I jumped about, barking my head off, my paws on the window sill, knocking over a vase of flowers and water which splayed over my head. A picture came crashing down and with it, the distinctive sound of shattering glass. This did not deter me from attempting to get out the window. I clumsily climbed up Toni's Hawaiian chair, wondering what on Earth had possessed my mistress to have such an ornate piece of furniture in the kitchen. Still, it served its purpose as an excellent climbing frame to get to my vantage point, where I could scrutinise my prey more carefully; for, miraculously, the cat was still where it fell. Was it dead? My thumping heart skipped a beat as my puzzled eyes waited patiently for some sign of movement. And then, after what seemed an eternity, it came. The moggy performed an act of resurrection as its, seconds ago, lifeless body arched and slowly, he rose, as his eyes looked warily around him, while his sleek, black fur stood on end. Whether that was due to the shock of the fall or the ferocious wind, we will never know; but, when its eyes met my eyes I could stand the tension no more. I needed to be outside. Now! Climbing further up, I was aware of bits of Hawaiian chair falling off. Don't ask me what pieces; I was in no mood to make a full examination of the collapsing structure and, to be absolutely honest with you, I'd rather not know. The infuriating cat was blatantly staring at me; teasing and toying with my instincts as if daring me to make a leap for him. And that's exactly what I did.

When I finally regained my consciousness, my poor head pounding, I cautiously raised myself and peered out the window. The feline was nowhere in sight; only the branches still performed their wild dance, stray bits of twigs and leaves travelling this way and that at the wind's discretion and all around me, a state of chaos.

I trembled inwardly at the sound of the howling wind outside; but that was nothing compared to the lecture I was dreading on Toni's return. Disheartened, defeated and frightened out of my wits, I lay my body alongside the upturned kitchen table and Hawaiian chair, the broken picture of Toni and myself in happier days, the shattered crystal vase which, on its way downwards, had the audacity to land on my head and the colourful flowers strewn around me. I lay my weary head on a solitary pink rose and awaited my fate. And surely it came.

The door slowly opened, as my heart beat frantically like a Hawaiian drum, and I desperately tried to feign sleep; for I had decided that to act completely innocent would be the best course of action. Of course, on later reflection, I realised this was a very bad choice. All I can say to add any credulity to the matter is that the bump on my head must have left me temporarily insane. Anyway, as I have mentioned, the door laboriously opened; for it was impossible to be opened smoothly with a variety of obstacles, not to mention my bulky self, in the way.

"What the dickens..."

I squeezed my eyes tightly; for I knew that tone of voice only too well and it did not give me a warm, glowing feeling. Cautiously, I opened one eye and saw the point of one black shoe trying to edge its way inside. I snapped my eye shut.

"Kamehameha... what on Earth...?" The door pushed arduously forward and more debris camouflaged my front paws, as the black polished shoe, with the hideous bow, eased inside and then the other shoe followed suit and I felt her full presence looming over me. What could I do? I scoured my fuddled brain furiously and came up with a right royal gesture. Picking up the somewhat flattened pink rose with my pearly whites, I sat bolt upright and presented it to my lady and that was the end of that episode. I was forgiven until…

To cut a very long story short, the wind, to my chagrin, decided not to ease up and neither did I, in my attempt to escape it. In my defence, I tried desperately, in my own way, to alert Toni to my fear by attempting to hide under the tablecloth, hoping that she would take the hint and do something about my plight. Perhaps, in hindsight, while she was tucking into her steak and kidney pie was not the ideal time; for she instantly opened the kitchen door and ushered me out and continued with her tea in peace. The weird and inexplicable thing is that outside, I had no fear of the wind. Anyway, suffice it to say, that while the wind reigned, Toni came home after a day's work to find disruption and mayhem, while I lay unconvincingly innocent in the midst of the mess.

It was on one such evening, when Toni had had enough of it all, and by *enough of it all* I mean that no amount of pink roses would appease her ruffled equilibrium, not to mention, her broken fragile nerves, she plonked herself down on her treasured Hawaiian chair, which now, thanks to Yours Truly, was held together by string and tape, and looked me squarely in the eyes and I knew, from past experiences, that this was going to be no fun. Usually my appealing, soulful eyes would soften her; but, today, they had lost their magic touch and I prepared myself for a full-scale lecture. What I heard tore my heart in shreds and, as I looked sadly on, trying silently to appeal to her better nature, she, in no uncertain terms, informed me of the consequences of my misdeeds.

In your wildest dreams, can you imagine how I felt at the sound of those incredulous words? Imagine a king on the verge of being deposed; removed from his own kingdom and that might give you an inkling. Surely, a tiny spark of hope told me, she was jesting. She had, after all, threatened me with similar punishments in the past, and here I am, as large as life and twice as beautiful. I dared to glance in her direction and wished I hadn't. The thunderous look on her face would make a mighty lion shrivel inside. No, this was no time for joking. I buried my head in my paws and pondered dismally on my future.

A life without Toni might, I mused, not be such a bad thing. For a start, I may have an entire house to roam about in and at my disposal instead of being consigned to the servant quarters, the kitchen, and though, I must confess, it is now a most elegant and modern kitchen, by right, I should be allowed in the more cosier areas like a nice cosy bedroom, with a king-sized bed with big, plush cushions suited to my royal status. Then there is the problem of constant treat rations, not to mention, muddy paws on a cleaned and highly polished floor and, as for the endless round of grooming which I absolutely detest; well, you know what I think about that nonsense. And, of course, I have to always try and be on my best behaviour, which is a bother when one yearns to be a bit mischievous now and again. Yes… maybe a change of home might not be such a bad thing after all. And, as I was about to ease into blissful sleep, a black thought crashed into my mind; for on one occasion, when I overdid it on the behaviour front, didn't Toni mention the sausage factory? My eyes flicked wide open and rested on the Judge of my Fate who, after a lengthy, and what seemed like a serious phone call, turned her serious eyes on me and stated determinedly, "Right, Kamehameha, I better get your things packed; tomorrow, you are going."

Going… going where, I yearned to ask her, to a nice home, perhaps, with lots of children to pamper me; my cousin, Suzi's house; a secluded, peaceful doggie sanctuary somewhere in the countryside; to the kennels; or to the… sausage factory? I searched her eyes but she was giving nothing away as she abruptly rose without a second glance thrown my way and started to feverishly pack all of my treats, my bedding, toys and food into one large black bin bag. All my worldly possessions thrown into an old bag and soon, I, and it, shall be disposed of. Can you imagine how someone of my royal status could feel? Well, I'll tell you. I felt like a good-for-nothing pooch who has lost his royal status and who has been reduced to the level of a lowly, homeless tramp. And as she vigorously collected my belongings, humming happily to herself; my heart sank lower and lower until I felt myself drowning in the depths of my own despair. For, hadn't I sometimes been a good pooch? Okay, I've been a bit naughty at times; but, haven't I brought joy, laughter and unexpected surprises (we won't mention the shocks) to Toni's otherwise dull existence? I know I haven't been the model pooch she may have wished for; but, haven't I lit up her life and prevented her from getting bored and old before her time? And what about the thousands of admiring glances, thrown our way, during our leisurely walks? Granted, they were all bestowed on me, rather than my mistress; but, I think she's beautiful even if nobody else thinks so. Doesn't all this count for anything? L looked across at her stern set face, her serious eyes not even wanting to glance my way, as she held open her black bag and threw in a juicy bone. My last meal, I dismally thought, as thoughts of the sausage factory loomed larger. And, after all that I had done for her. Didn't I, after all, save our castle from flooding and what about the time I dutifully posed in Hawaiian leis for her guests to admire, although, I must secretly admit, I did revel in the adulation? Oh yes, and what about the countless suitors I vetted for my mistress? Obviously, all these incidents are now forgotten as she continued in her determined mission to get rid of me.

Dejected, rejected, sad and somewhat depressed, I watched her scurrying around, collecting everything associated with me and throwing it into the black bag. It's a wonder, I glumly thought, she doesn't stick me in there and throw me into the garbage bin. A spontaneous smile broke within me as I remembered the incident with the bin and the garbage. Oh so very long ago now… If only I hadn't been such a naughty pooch. Now I have an old age of misery and squalor to look forward to and, what's more, the wind is picking up again. Time to hide; under the tablecloth I go, and there, neither of us have to look at the other while my heart breaks into a thousand pieces for the things, and the one human, I love in this world.

I dared to peep from beneath the tablecloth just once and once was more than enough, as I saw Toni's eyes staring coldly at my makeshift sanctuary, while the wind outside howled and whistled and made me tremble all over; but even that was nothing compared to the dread building up inside of me; dread and fear of the unknown. It was in these minutes of deep desperation that my ultimate fate was sealed.

The fury of the nights wind ceased. Dawn broke and, as I peeped out from under the tablecloth, I saw my mistress's determined feet; heard the rustle of the bin bag as it was clenched into her hand and the stern command, "Kamehameha!" Reluctantly, I crept out of my hiding place and faced bravely my fate.

Without a sound, apart from the soft purring of the engine, we sat side by side as the car slid out of the drive and sometime later slid into another drive; one I was vaguely familiar with for I had been here before. So, this was going to be my new home. My eyes looked around as I read the bold sign, Heavenly Home Kennels, as thoughts of my previous stay came crashing into my head and soon disappeared as I heard her swift command, "Come on, Kamehameha," her voice cold, shrill and detached. The exchange was brief. One minute she was there conversing with the kennel owners; the next, the car and she were gone.

So this was it. This was my future. This is where I was to spend my final days. My eyes drifted from pen to pen, as my ears took in the array of doggie sounds emitting from each pen. Where were the playful Alsatian and the stuck-up, self-obsessed Poodle; no doubt living life to the full in their luxurious homes?

Still, I concluded, it could have been worse; it could have been the sausage factory. With a deep sigh and a firm resolve to be good at all times, I followed my keeper into my new home.

That night was the worst night of my life. I lay awake thinking of what I had lost through my own stupidity; a nice comfortable home, a mistress I could twist around my paw, treats, adventures, nice meals, a lovely garden to play in, and, above all, my royal status. For am I not 'King' Kamehameha? Am I not named after a very important, great king of an island far, far away? And now I am a nobody; another dog amongst dogs; just another number disposed of and forgotten. And what was Toni up to? I wondered. Probably throwing a party; a Hawaiian party with her mates to mark her happy release from me, revelling in the fact that she would no longer need to take me for walks in all kinds of weather; not to mention the money she would save and, of course, her precious kitchen floor would now always be sparkling clean. Yes, she would be rejoicing in the fact that I was no longer a part of her life; but, I… well, I already miss her like I have never missed another, because she was everything to me: my mistress, my provider and my one true friend. With a heart full of heavy conflicting emotions, I fell into a restless and fitful sleep, not caring if I woke up again; unconscious to the fact that my one true friend was having a sleepless night of her own; for, in a spontaneous bid to teach me a lesson in behaviour, she found herself in her own den of loneliness and misery. Unable to find sanctuary in sleep, Toni sauntered downstairs to make herself a mug of coco and, while the milk was heating up in the pan, her exhausted eyes darted to my sleeping quarters, where she had earlier replaced my bedding with an elegant tall vase, boasting extravagant tropical blooms and her heart broke into a thousand pieces, as she closed her eyes and pondered. What was he doing? Was he adapting well to his new surroundings? Was he cold… happy… sad… lonely… frightened… did he miss her as much as her heart broke for him? As his soulful eyes haunted her thoughts, her eyes flicked open to the over-boiled milk. Abandoning the drink, she hastened up the stairs two at a time, ran into her bedroom, flung open the wardrobe doors, dug her hands into the deep recesses of the interior and brought out a thick wad of silky material. Stroking her fingers along the luxurious fabric, she mused regretfully. It would have made a most elegant Mother Hubbard for her next Hawaiian evening. Still… Frantically, she gathered up the material, together with her rushing thoughts, and sat down at the sowing machine, with one magnificent thought firmly in her mind as a happy smile, the first one to grace her face for a long time, settled delightedly on her humming lips.

The sight which greeted me… well let me tell you about it. I opened one eye and was absolutely convinced I was dreaming; for I saw one highly polished black shoe standing right before my nose. Cautiously, I opened my other eye and there they were; two highly polished black shoes which I recognised immediately. For who, in their right mind, apart from one person, would have two ghastly, oversized bows on the front. I averted my eyes from the distasteful articles and, as my eyes rose up the plump legs and up… up… up they came eye to eye with Toni, making my fast-pounding heart stop momentarily and restart its furious beating with a surge of undiluted joy. This was no dream. Here she was, in a hideous tweed skirt, with a fussy, odious blouse and a smile as wide as the Grand Canyon, bestowed on me. I blinked and blinked again and felt her soft podgy arms around my neck and I felt I was in pure heaven.

"Come on, Kamehameha."

I didn't need to be asked twice, though inwardly, I must confess, though I am highly intelligent, on this occasion I was truly bemused. What was all this caper about? In less than an hour, I found out.

Gingerly, I placed one paw in front of the other and walked into the dreaded kitchen and there I stood totally transfixed, my disbelieving eyes glued hypnotically to the vision before me, my heart beating wildly as my senses reeled with a thousand emotions. I heard the echo of a concerned voice. "Don't you like it, Kamehameha?"

Like it… I love it!

I stepped towards the object I was staring at, my eyes momentarily staring back at a beaming Toni, and stepped boldly inside, into a luxurious den fit for a king, with big silky cushions and a rich tropical silky drape around. What a hideout! (Thoughts of King Kamehameha's hideout, on one of the Hawaiian Islands, crashed into my mind.) Immediately I wasted no precious time and made myself comfortable on an oversized plush cushion, feeling very much the sovereign I knew I looked. Now the ferocious wind could come and go and, I knew, I was safe and secure. My faithful eyes rested on my mistress, my true friend. Mahalo, I said silently. I shall never be naughty again, I promised, until… the next time and her warm, happy smile told me she loved me… unconditionally.

Chapter Nineteen
Happy Days

And so, to reflect on my life; it's been a good life from pup to my present-day status; yes, it's been a good, happy life.

I know, initially, I was far from impressed with my name; but, as I reflect, I can honestly conclude that it's been a blessing in disguise because with my name came a lot of unexpected privileges. The name, Kamehameha, has certainly made me feel different; a pooch apart from all other pooches; for already I am, in some mysterious way, associated with a romantic, tropical island thousands of kilometres away and, to add to my important status, my namesake is none other than the Great King Kamehameha of Hawaii; because of all this, I have always behaved in a rather aloof manner; a manner that portrays both wisdom and gracefulness and a great deal of superiority.

I know I was a bit of a pain when I first arrived on the scene, for example, chewing Toni's chairs and doors was not one of my brilliant moves, but then, what was a pup supposed to do when his gums are itching like crazy? Stealing the string of Polish sausages was wrong, I know; but, would any level headed pooch resist such temptation? Snatching my mistress's ghastly, oversized knickers off the line; well, the less said about that episode, the better. Setting out to explore the big, wide world was, perhaps, overdoing things a little and certainly did not win Toni over; but, in the end, we both recovered and all that vigorous searching for me probably boosted her fitness regime. Creating delightful fountains in the hosepipe, that was pure, undiluted fun and I can't wait for the next blissful opportunity. Anyway, my excuse for these little foibles of mine is that Toni would certainly have a dull life without me; so, really I'm doing her a great favour when I constantly keep her on her toes.

Fireworks, I shall never, ever, get used to and, as far as I am concerned, they should be banned from the face of the Earth. To this very day, their bangs, whizzes and whistles make me tremble to the very core of my being and leave me feeling as if I'm in the throes of Armageddon which, after some reflection, would probably be a better option.

Rules, regulations and dealing with my own, personal Sergeant Major do not thrill me at all; but, what can a pooch do in my predicament? I have come to the quick conclusion that I must avoid, where possible; if not avoidable, grin and bear it, switch off and dream about sausages.

Visitors are always welcome, as long as they arrive bearing interesting, edible gifts. Most of them come armed with a generous supply; the one or two who barely escape with their lives intact, know exactly what to do on their next visit, should they venture to call again.

My cousin, Suzi; now, there's a problem. She's a blot on the landscape; a fiend in the guise of a cute pooch. I have tried several times to get on the good side of her: sharing, flirting, frolicking, even dating, to name but a few, but all attempts have failed miserably. I must admit, I did actually think there was a glimmer of hope when she rescued me from my watery grave; but, that was short-lived and, before we knew it, we were back to our old ways and that's how, I think, it's going to stay. My only request to my Greater Power is that I shall be preserved from encountering her in doggie Heaven, not that she has a hope in aspiring to reach such dizzy heights; so, I think, I'm pretty safe from that particular fate.

One fate I shall never be successful in avoiding is Toni's obsession with that far flung island, Hawaii, and its effect on me, why even the v—e—t rolls his eyes at my name call. To my utter embarrassment, I've heard him chuckle. "K… Ka. Maya… m… sorry, Miss Lublinska… ho… ho…" Honestly, I have to put up with this kind of nonsense in front of my peers!

There is no get out clause concerning the Hawaiian evenings, which never fail to follow Toni's vacation to the islands and, if I have any hope of being treated like a king, then I have to put up and shut up; such is life!

We are now into early October and I can feel the chill in the air; the days seem shorter and autumn is well and truly on its way as we enter the last quarter of the year. Like the leaves, which were once green, lush and full of life and are now beginning to change to orange and yellow and fall to the ground, I feel a change. No longer can I run so fast; though, I can still give Toni a run for her money; no longer can I rise so agilely; though, it's surprising how fast I can miraculously rise when I smell a tasty treat nearby and, maybe, I cannot see so clearly; but, don't even think of putting me out to pasture; for, I have a lot of life left in this body and a lot more adventures to live. I have got no intention of leaving Toni anytime soon, for how would she be able to cope without me? I have no intention of quitting; for, if anything, I have to keep my mistress on her toes, lest she get old before her time. It is my job to keep her young in spirit, if not in looks. So, I'm staying and long may I reign!

A Final Note from the King

I think, by now, you have probably got the picture. Between you and me, I must admit, I am a very happy pooch. Toni, my mistress, is not a bad 'old' stick and I've almost got her into thinking she's the boss, whereas, in fact, you and I know better.

I've got a good life, in fact, a five-star luxury life style; although, I'm not daft, I wouldn't allow Toni to think that she is spoiling me too much; I know the consequences of that particular admission. But, you know, she's all right as far as owners go and, I'm glad to say, I've got her where I want her… most of the time; the other five percent of the time I'm still working on.

I like our single status; for, I am only too aware that if one or other; or, both of us find a mate one, or both of us, would miss out; so, I guess, it's the single life for us both. We shall, no doubt, put up with each other's idiosyncrasies and rub along together quite nicely.

As far as I am concerned, when I weigh it all up: all the ups and downs of daily life, the smiles and frowns, the good times and the bad, the adventures, escapades, disaster, fears, joys, rules and regulations; when I've had time to assess all, and to adapt everything I possibly can to my advantage, I think I'm on to a good thing and I ask myself the question: why on Earth would I ever dream of leaving in search of better things? For I know, without a doubt, I could search the world over, and after years of traversing thousands of kilometres, I know in my heart of hearts, I would never find another Toni, who would allow me to live my life as 'King' Kamehameha!

A Note from the Faithful Servant

Kamehameha! What can I say? He likes to think he's the boss; though, obviously we all know the true identity of the ultimate sovereign in our castle.

He is frustrating, annoying disobedient at times, often leaves his post when he's scheduled to be on duty; spoilt, playful, delightful, funny, loyal when he wants to be, cunning and highly intelligent all wrapped up in a lovely big, fluffy ball; that is, when he cares to be groomed and spruced up.

You can imagine what I have to put up with. He has given you a fairly accurate description of proceedings; however, I must add that he's sprinkled some accounts with a generous amount of exaggeration, and a great deal of self-glorification, on more than one occasion. I shall let you, the reader, assess and formulate the truth for yourself.

This cuddly pooch of mine has embarrassed me more than once; the incident concerning my oversized pants on Mister Frobisher's pole immediately springs to mind; though, I must admit, to his credit, he has also saved the day as in the event of the kitchen floor flooding episode; so, you see, somehow he always manages to make up for his misdeeds and all ends up being forgiven; he is left feeling the ultimate hero, leaving me to feel as if I should be eternally grateful for his forward thinking and shining intelligence.

I am sure he thinks life was very dull for me before he arrived on the scene and certainly, I must agree. In his company, one can never be expected to experience a dull moment. Life would be more sedate and less ruffled without him; though I must admit, but not to him, it would not be the same; for, if he left, he would take with him fun, humour and a great deal of spontaneous sparkle.

When I think back to some of the times we have had together: the Hawaiian evenings, the lake episode, his over indulging with the Polish sausages, Halloween, Bonfire Night, Christmas, the kitchen renovations; not to mention episodes with potential suitors, I can't help but smile, because, as day surely follows night; happiness always follows frustration... eventually.

So, as he saunters into our new, modern kitchen and sits by my side, looking high and mighty, I put my arms around his fluffy, soft neck and bring him closer to myself.

"Kamehameha." I sigh resignedly, as he nudges closer to me. "You truly are the 'king' of our castle!"